this
time
around

finding love in scotland

book 2

gina azzi

This Time Around

Copyright © 2019 by Gina Azzi

Disclaimer: *This Time Around* is a second chance, single dad romance. It contains sensitive topics including domestic abuse and sexual assault. It is intended for mature audiences.

1

aaron

"Is your goal in life to be celibate forever?" My brother Finn's eyes gleam with amusement. The irritating kind because it's at my expense.

"What are you talking about?" I slice Olivia's apple into pieces, adding it to the third compartment on her kid's lunch plate.

"That's what you're wearing to the Fringe?"

"What's wrong with this?" I glance down at my jeans and white button-down, the sleeves rolled up on my forearms.

"It's worse than I thought." Finn directs his observation toward his girlfriend, Daisy, as she and my daughter race into the kitchen for lunch.

They're giggling and swatting at each other, and some of the anger binding my ribs and oozing into the cavity of my chest lessens with Olivia's smile. Seeing Livvy laugh again is healing, like a salve to the guilt I've been carrying around since Kate and I divorced six months ago.

"Here you go, Livvy." I place her lunch plate and

water bottle in front of her place setting, taking an extra moment to appreciate that she's here, in my kitchen, with me. Her mother had her in Paris for the entire month of July, and between Kate's narcissistic tendencies and her lover's apathetic life outlook, my daughter returned home a different person.

In one short summer, Olivia transformed from a bubbly, energetic seven-year-old into a withdrawn, uninterested stranger. One glance into Liv's sad eyes has my blood pressure spiking, my anger toward Kate clouding all rational thought. *Why the hell did she have to ruin our family? Why is she putting Olivia through this much heartache at such a tender age?*

I can't allow Kate's shortcomings to affect Olivia any more than they already have. Now that my daughter is back in Scotland, I need to make sure she knows she has one parent she can count on; that she's my top priority and sole focus.

"Thanks, Daddy." She gifts me a sweet smile, her pigtails falling forward as she drops her head to bite into the sandwich I prepared for her.

"What's worse than you thought?" Daisy asks Finn, and he turns, gesturing toward me.

Daisy bites back a chuckle, her gaze sweeping over me. "Aar, you know I think you're pretty amazing, but you can't wear that to the Fringe."

"What's wrong with it?"

"It's too serious. This is a music festival for creatives, a celebration of individuality. We're taking

Olivia to see the street performers, enjoy some kid shows. Don't you have anything more... fun?"

"Fun?"

"Yeah, you know... like a T-shirt?"

Finn snorts his laughter, loud and obnoxious.

I glare at him, and he holds up his hands for a second before wrapping an arm around Daisy's waist and tugging her against his frame. "Don't get ornery, mate. We're trying to help you." He glances at Olivia before mouthing to me, "Get laid."

"What does Daddy need help with?" Olivia asks curiously, missing nothing.

"His fashion sense," Finn tells her seriously.

"Oh." She looks at me. "I like how you look, Daddy."

"That's good, Liv, since your opinion is the only one I care about."

"Just... a T-shirt, okay?" Daisy tries again. "More casual."

Blowing out a deep breath, I yank on the back of my neck. I know Finn and Daisy have my best interests at heart, at least what they think are my best interests. They want to see me going out to blow-off steam, open to dating, maybe even actually dating. They want to know that I'm moving on from my divorce, letting go of some of the anger and bitterness that eats at my stomach like acid.

But fuck, it's hard. Everything reminds me of Kate. Songs on the radio, ties I wore to special occasions, an

Italian restaurant I pass on my way to work each morning. And every single thing I connect to her causes the swell of fury over the destruction she caused to expand. And the anguish I feel over my own failures to multiply.

When the hell is the growing bubble of disappointment going to pop?

Kate ruined too much. She stole a piece of my heart, a chunk of Olivia's innocence, and ground them between her fingers until they disintegrated into nothingness.

And now, there's nothing left for me to give to any female, unless her name is Olivia.

Meeting my brother and his girlfriend's expectant gazes, I blow out a breath, like air leaking from a balloon, defeated. "A T-shirt."

"Thank God," Finn mutters as Daisy lets out a "Hallelujah."

"Today is going to be fun," Daisy calls after me as I leave the kitchen and walk down the hallway to my bedroom to change.

I raise a hand in acknowledgement, unsure if I even know how to have fun anymore.

THE FRINGE IS A PRETTY big deal.

With more than 50,000 performances spanning three

weeks on stages all across Edinburgh, The Fringe is a massive celebration of the arts in all forms—dance, theater, comedy, music, etc. Tourists and festival-goers flock to the city, overwhelming Edinburgh with traffic and litter in addition to individuality and creativity. It's a pretty awesome time and it reinvigorates my perspective as a marketing executive at one of the biggest firms in the UK.

Walking down the Royal Mile, Olivia's attention swings frantically from one street performance to the next. Bright colors, vivid patterns, and loud noises wrap us up in a creative bubble buzzing with energy.

"Look, Daddy," She points at a dragon, the mask twisting and turning in beat to a thumping bass.

"That's pretty awesome." I squeeze her small hand in mine.

"I'm going to grab a program for the children's shows. Maybe we can catch one while we're here." Daisy points to an information booth.

"Okay, we'll be around here."

It's hot today, the sun pounding on our backs. Frowning, I shift Olivia's hat on her head. *Does she need another coat of sun cream? Did I even remember to bring the sun cream?* "Olivia, drink some water." I shake a water bottle under her nose, relieved when she takes a few sips before squealing as the dragon breathes fire.

Patting her head, I drop her water bottle into my backpack and falter, my gaze landing on a beautiful woman. A thousand memories slam into me as I take her in, my heart galloping in my chest.

Is it her?

She's stunning, effortlessly so. The type of lovely one reads about but rarely experiences. Unassuming yet ethereal. Clad in cut-off denim shorts, fringes dangle several inches down her tanned, toned thighs. A flimsy, light pink tank top shows off her shoulders as strands of silver and gold necklaces decorate her slender neck, throwing the sunlight like a prism.

Something about the way she moves, languidly yet purposeful, like all five of her senses are engaged, soaking up the energy pulsing around her, has me stepping in her direction.

Everly Pierce.

Her petite frame, her shiny brown hair falling in waves around her shoulders, and her sun-kissed skin fills the space of my chest up with awareness, a familiarity that brings more hope than it should.

Is it her?

Why is she here?

She glances up then, as if she heard my silent question, and her eyes slam into mine.

Green—a mixture of sage and moss and olive—a shade so unforgettable, it's imprinted in my mind, even though nearly fifteen years have passed since I've seen her.

Her mouth drops open, full lips I once kissed, parting in shock as confusion ripples over her expression. She shakes her head the slightest bit, and the jewelry around her neck shimmers. Wide eyes bleeding with recognition scan my face, searching for confirmation that it's me, here, now. She takes a step forward, as if on auto-pilot, and stumbles, the ground rushing up to meet her.

"Everly." Placing Olivia's hand in Finn's, I bolt toward her.

2
♫ everly 🎤

One glance into Aaron Anderson's cerulean eyes shocks my system, causing me to literally trip over air.

My heart rate spikes, each beat tripping over the last, like a sprinter who's taken too many months off. The sticky heat coating the back of my neck spreads, slow and thick, like molasses moving through my veins. My palms grow clammy, my eyes widen, and I freeze. But really, how could I not?

It's Aaron freaking Anderson.

The first boy to properly kiss me.

Not sweet and safe like the other boys, but thoroughly and with intention. Like he'd consume me if I tried to pull away.

The first man to break my heart. Not slowly, chipping at its edges, but suddenly and all at once, so it shattered.

I haven't seen him in nearly fifteen years, but, if I'm being honest, he crosses my mind a hell of a lot more than an ex-boyfriend should. Just watching him move closer, mouthing my name, has my heart scrambling up my throat and my stomach flipping in anticipation. Clearly, my body hasn't forgotten the touch of Aaron, even though my most recent ex, Corey, toiled tirelessly to erase any trace of him during our four years together.

As if I could ever forget Aaron Anderson.

As if I'd want to.

"Everly?" Aaron's voice jolts through me and warms my chest, as if from muscle memory. "Is it really you? Are you all right?"

Dragging my eyes up slowly, I know what's coming. Yep. Once my gaze collides with his, the music festival, the hundreds of people and rowdy street performers, and the swatches of blinding color fades away and Aaron Anderson—the concern shadowing his irises, his muscled, corded forearm leading to his strong hand that gently touches my ankle as he crouches down beside me —consumes me.

God, he's still perfect.

His strong, unyielding jawline, clean-shaven and smooth, tightens as concern deepens the color of his bright, blue eyes. His dark blond hair is freshly cut and neatly styled with a touch of grey starting at his temples. I grin, the ridiculous amount of time separating us becoming too apparent as I drink in his subtle changes. A tiny scar underneath his left eyebrow, the starker angles of his face, all man now. *Does the dimple in his left cheek still pop when he chuckles?*

Stop it! He's probably married by now. He must

be. There's no way his ass wasn't snapped off the market about five seconds after he ended things with you.

"Daddy?" a small voice hovers near his shoulder, drowning out my mental musings.

My eyes swing toward the voice, landing on an adorable little girl with large blue eyes and two neat braids, like Dorothy in the *Wizard of Oz*.

"Livvy, this is an old friend of mine. Everly Pierce," Aaron answers, tucking the little girl under his arm, even though his eyes never leave mine.

"You're a father?" I blurt, smacking my palm against my mouth in embarrassment.

Aaron chuckles, his dimple flashes, and I grin. "Sorry." I shake my head, turning my attention to his daughter. "It's nice to meet you Livvy."

She tilts her head, her eyes growing even larger. "I know you."

"You do?" I cock my head to the side, squinting against the blinding sunlight. Apparently, I managed to lose my sunglasses in my tumble. #Winning.

Her face grows solemn as she nods.

Oh God, did Aaron tell her about me? About us?

No, that makes no sense. Why would he do that?

Gah! Did he tell his wife?

But what would she say? Back in college, your dad had an American girlfriend.

Girlfriend.

Is that all I was? No, we were so much more.

Together, Aaron Anderson and I were... #relationshipgoals.

Weren't we?

He has a family now, Everly. Move on.

"Aye. You sing that song Daisy likes." Livvy hums the tune to my most recent single, "Mending Broken."

Aaron whips his head toward his daughter.

"You're right," I laugh, clapping. "I think your friend Daisy has pretty good taste."

"Daisy is Uncle Finn's girlfriend. She always lets me try on her perfume and nail varnish."

"She sounds awesome."

Livvy nods, glancing at her father. "You're friends with her? She's like, famous."

I chuckle as Aaron's eyebrows bend in surprise, the corners of his mouth ticking up at his daughter.

But when his eyes swing back to me, they're a raging storm of complicated mixed with skepticism heated with desire. The cerulean has been stamped out by sapphire, the edges of his irises blazing like the hottest part of a flame.

His mouth curves into the shadow of a smile and I nearly groan, pinching myself to stay in the present. Aaron is a family man now, not still living in the memories of a college relationship like a crazy person.

Ahem, me.

But, be still my beating heart, his eyes. They're shipwreck eyes and Jesus, it scares me how desperately a part of me wants to drown in them.

Standing from Livvy's side, he offers me a hand and tugs me upward.

"Oh fuck. God, I'm sorry!" I wail, bending to grip my ankle as pain rips through my leg.

"Where does it hurt, Lee?" His voice is low and commanding and the effortless way my nickname, the one that only he ever called me, rolls off his tongue soothes the part of me that never got over him.

"Ankle. I think I sprained it." My ankle throbs now that I'm upright with all of my blood pooling to my feet. Balancing on my right foot, I lift my left off the ground and teeter until Aaron wraps his large hand around my upper arm.

At his touch, my skin burns and chills, a shudder radiating throughout my body. His breath catches, but I don't look at him, knowing if I do, it will be too much. Too overwhelming. He was always too much for me to handle.

Once upon a time, hell, even five seconds ago, I wanted nothing more than to drown in the deep blue pools of his gaze. Now, I know better, and you better believe I'm reaching for that life preserver—my sanity depends on it.

Stay strong, Everly. Stay the course.

"I got you."

Gah! I waver. "Is your wife here too?"

Glancing up at him, a thousand unspoken words between us, I watch as his lips press into a thin line, his

Adam's apple bobbing once. He shakes his head, "Not in the picture." He murmurs, his eyes bleeding with too many emotions for me to decipher. He looks away quickly and gestures to someone over my head.

"Hey, there you are." A friendly voice with a Scottish brogue nowhere near as thick as Aaron's, calls out. Moments later, a tall guy with the same bright blue eyes as Aaron's and Livvy's arrives and places a hand on Livvy's shoulder. "Everything all right?"

"This is Everly. She's a singer Daisy likes. And Daddy knows her. And she sprained her ankle," Livvy summarizes, her eyes darting from her father to me to the newcomer who can only be Aaron's brother, given the resemblance between them.

"Woah, Olivia! You run away from me and meet a famous singer? How is this going to teach you not to run off?" Finn grins down at his niece.

"You ran away from Uncle Finn?" Aaron scowls.

"Sorry Daddy."

Finn clears his throat, earning an apology from Olivia that causes his grin to widen. "All good, little love." Cutting his gaze to me, he lifts his chin slightly. "Hey, Finn Anderson. You okay?"

"Just a sprain." I wave a hand, trying to hobble out of Aaron's grasp. Trying to absorb that tiny detail that landed like an anvil: his wife is not in the picture. Where is she? Shaking my head, I manage a smile. "I'm Everly."

Aaron's grip on my arm tightens, his fingertips like embers. Finn's eyes narrow, catching the movement and he glances at Aaron.

"Everly and I attended the same uni that semester I was in America." Aaron supplies.

A flicker of recognition sparks in Finn's gaze, and he rolls his lips together, pinning them between his teeth. Rocking back on his heels, he crosses his arms before chuckling softly. "Good to meet you."

"Likewise," I reply. "Anyway, y'all enjoy the festival. I'm sorry to intrude on your time like this." Pulling my cell phone from the back pocket of my cut offs, I wave it around, chuckling at my misfortune. "I'm going to call my ride. Good to see you, Aaron. And good meeting y'all." I offer Livvy a genuine smile and she beams back. She's freaking adorable. But, of course, Aaron would have a cute kid.

"So, I'm going to take her to the hospital. You don't mind keeping Liv?" Aaron talks over my head.

"Aaron, really, I'm fine." I yank on my arm, exasperated.

Why do men always think that they have to fix things? And that the way to do so is by ignoring the woman's wishes? I'm not exactly a damsel in distress. I'm more than capable of —

"Lee, please. Let me make sure you're okay." Aaron's voice is firm, unyielding. I open my mouth to explain that I already am okay, but he cuts me a look that forces me to swallow my words.

Not because I'm scared of standing up to him. He's not Corey.

But because his look is fire hot, heady and blazing, unbalanced and desperate.

It's needy and my entire being jolts to life as his gaze caresses me the way I wish his hands would.

Be still my heart.

Stay strong, Everly. Stay the course.

"'Course not. We'll have a blast. Roger called, and he's swinging by with Gerry in a bit."

"Thanks, mate." Aaron slides his hand down my arm, his fingers clasping my wrist, as he crouches down in front of his daughter. He speaks to her quietly and she nods, her braids bopping up and down. Balancing on my good foot, the trail of Aaron's fingers down my arm cause jolts of electricity to shimmy through my veins, and I close my eyes, reveling in my body's reaction to him and hating it at the same time.

Aaron is supposed to be in the past.

But God does it feel good to stand beside him again.

"Feel better, Ms. Everly," Livvy says, waving as she disappears into the swell of festival-goers with her uncle.

Aaron shifts his weight next to me, his fingers lacing with mine so naturally, it aches that it's not an everyday occurrence. "God, it's good to see you, Lee."

Nodding, I step closer, automatically pulled toward him. Completely forgetting about my ankle, I yelp as the pain from my fall washes over me and both legs give out. Gravity pulls Aaron and I to the ground where we land in a heap, surrounded by hundreds of people, in the middle of the Royal Mile.

3

aaron

H er body is pressed against mine in all the right places, and I swallow back a groan.

Why the hell am I still acting like a twenty-two-year-old uni student around her?

And how has she not changed at all?

Shapely, athletic legs with shorts that barely cover her ass, a slim waist framed by wicked curves, and a smile that could melt a glacier. My body begins to respond to her heat, her presence, her goddamn sunshine, and I curse, angry with my traitorous limbs and wayward thoughts when Everly is clearly in pain.

But Jesus, if she doesn't look like salvation and sin procreated. Her chest heaves, drawing my attention to the perky firmness of her breasts. One of the tiny straps of her shirt slips off her shoulder and I nearly groan again. Looping a finger around the material, I drag it back up her arm, painfully aware of how damn soft her skin is.

Standing quickly, I reach down again and help her up.

We pause, staring at each other, as a loaded pause colors the space between us.

"Everly —"

"Aar—"

Both of us chuckle as Everly shakes her head, her long hair brushing across the tops of her attention-stealing breasts.

Pull yourself together, mate.

You need to get Everly to the damn hospital.

Stop thinking about her incredible breasts and how they would taste if —

Everly winces, the color seeping out of her cheeks and I shut down my desperate thoughts and focus on the woman in front of me. Drawn to her brilliant green eyes, a pang cuts through my chest that I can't read them anymore.

"You don't have to do this. I can call my ride."

I shake my head, hanging onto her elbow as I guide her toward my car. "How's the pain?"

"Manageable." She murmurs, the toe of her moccasin snagging on a dip in the pavement. "Shit."

"Here." I shift, wrapping an arm around her waist, my hand palming her stomach. "Put your weight on me."

She stops abruptly, her entire body locking down.

"Everly?"

She doesn't move, her body stiff and unyielding. Her eyes are unfocused, like she's in a trance and her breathing stutters.

"Lee?" I say louder and she glances up. Wariness rings her irises, and a flicker of unease zips through me. "I'm just trying to help you. I don't want to make you uncomfortable."

She nods again, her eyes growing shiny in the sunlight. An unexpected layer of moisture collects in her eyes, surprising and concerning the hell out of me. "I know."

"You're in pain, babe." I swing her up into my arms, hooking one arm under her knees, the other cradling her against my chest.

"Aaron! What? Put me down."

"It's faster this way." I stride forward, taking a shortcut down a side street.

"I'm too heavy."

I snort, glancing down at her.

"I'm serious," she protests, a small smile fluttering over her full lips, even though she seems anxious.

"I forgot how serious you can be. We're almost to my car."

Sighing, she closes her eyes and rests her head against my chest. A small smile flits across her mouth as she listens to my heartbeat, and the realization that that's what she's doing only accelerates it.

When we arrive at my car, I place her down gently, opening the passenger door, and helping her slide inside and buckle in. Rounding the back of the car to the driver's side, I steel myself for being in such a confined space with Everly. Everything about her is effortless.

She's the only woman who ever tied me up in knots and cut them free at the same time.

Starting my car, I glance over to find her staring directly at me, her shoulders squared, her eyes curious.

"How are you doing?" I flip the ignition.

"Hanging in there."

"Are you just in town just for the festival?"

"I'm not sure."

"Why are you here, Everly?"

"Just hiding out."

My hands slide from the steering wheel as I turn the ignition off. Unease unfurls in my veins as irrational thoughts trickle through my mind. *Hiding out? From who? Did someone hurt her?* "What?"

"Just taking a breather, a time-out from my life."

"Why?"

"It's complicated." She shrugs, but the way she averts her gaze, letting her hair fall forward and creating a barrier between us, bothers me.

Opening my mouth to ask more questions, I bite back down on my tongue when Everly angles her body closer to the window, away from me.

"Well, if you need anything while you're in Scotland, call me, yeah?"

She nods, the silky strands of her hair rippling against her back, but she doesn't turn her head. "Sure."

"WHAT ARE YOU LOOKING AT? Do I have something on my face?" She wrinkles her nose, sitting next to me in the hospital waiting room, her fingers gripping the arm rests.

"No, it's not that."

"What is it?"

"Just surprised, I guess. That it's really you."

"It's just lil' ol' me." She lifts her hands and flutters her fingers.

"Just lil' ol' you, huh? You seem different."

"It's been almost fifteen years, Aaron. Of course I'm different."

"I know. It's just strange. In so many ways, it's like you haven't changed and yet, so much time has passed."

"I know what you mean." She grins at me. "You look good, Aar. Like you've barely aged at all."

Laughing, I shake my head, pointing to my temples. "Have you missed my grey hair?"

"It's distinguished."

"It's being a full-time dad."

Everly's face falls. "I'm sorry. I didn't realize that —"

"We divorced. Six months ago."

"Shit, Aaron. That sucks. I'm sorry things didn't work out."

"Me too. Mostly for Olivia."

"She seems incredible."

"She is." I scrub a palm over my chin. "She's the most important person in the world to me."

"I bet you're an amazing dad." Her voice sounds wistful and she's watching me with a longing that stirs old memories, forgotten emotions, to life.

"Everly, I —"

"Everly Pierce." The receptionist calls out.

I stand beside her, my hand on her elbow as I guide her toward the receptionist. "I can come with you."

She freezes, her eyes widening as she looks up at me.

"You may need the support," the receptionist throws out helpfully.

Finally, Everly nods, and we follow the receptionist into an empty unit in triage.

Everly slides onto the hospital bed and stuffs a pillow underneath her ankle, elevating it. I take the chair by her bedside.

For a handful of long seconds, the only sound between us is our breaths mixing, feeling each other out, separating the past from the present, hurt from possibility.

"Why here?" I ask, breaking the silence.

"Edinburgh?"

"Aye. You could have taken a break from your life and gone anywhere. What made you choose Scotland?"

"Someone I used to know once told me it's magic," she quips, her look meaningful.

God, I remember the night she's referring to, the Tennessee whiskey we drank on a rooftop, the stars that seemed bright enough to touch, falling down around us like a dream.

"Someone you used to know, huh?"

"Yeah. He was an exchange student. Gorgeous blue eyes and a smile bright enough to rival the sun. His accent was the talk of my entire dorm floor, only second to his ripped body."

I chuckle, knowing she's messing with me. "What happened?"

"He made me believe in beautiful things. And then he broke my heart." Her voice cracks and my eyes jump to hers, but I can't read them. Can't read her and it pisses me off, serving as another reminder of my failures.

I never should have let her go.

Inhaling sharply, my chest tightens at her lost expression. Raking my teeth over my lips, I yank the back of my neck.

What the hell do I say to that?

I did break her heart. I knew it before I did it, and I had to live with it afterwards. But the hurt flaring in her eyes is as unexpected as seeing her at The Fringe.

"I never meant to hurt you, Lee. Not the way I did," I confess, the binding in my chest growing unbearable. In a way, it's a relief to know my heart isn't permanently damaged after the blender Kate's had it in for the past year.

She offers me a sweet, sad smile, her fingers playing

with the strands of gold and silver at the base of her throat. "I know."

"But you still came. Here. To my city."

"Maybe I'm searching for some magic."

"You going to write a song about it?" I joke, desperate to lighten the atmosphere and cut the undercurrent of tension between us. Because if Everly doesn't perk up soon, I'm going to be forced to fist the hem of her shirt and drag my lips across hers.

My fingers are already itching to reach out and touch her. The realization scares me as much as it soothes.

"Maybe."

I shift forward in my chair, dropping my elbows to my knees. "You really did it then? You're a famous singer?"

Her mouth drops open, an adorable snort slipping from her nose. "Aaron, at the risk of sounding completely self-absorbed, do you not know who I am?"

"Know who you are?" Olivia's declaration that Everly sings a song Daisy likes flickers through my mind. "You're Everly Pierce, treasurer of Vanderbilt's freshman class, aspiring singer, soulful songwriter, and lover of mac and cheese and Tennessee bourbon."

A real laugh bursts from her mouth as she grins. "Fair enough. I once was all those things. And look, I know country music isn't a huge thing over here but... have you not followed me at all?"

"Not really."

"Why not?" Her cheeks redden, embarrassed, and I see her again, the tempest I once loved. God, I've missed her without ever knowing just how much.

"I followed you in the beginning. I knew you signed with a label and were going to give music a shot. I don't know much beyond that. Seeing you living a life—a different one than what I envisioned for us—it hurt too much."

"You do remember that you broke up with me, right?"

"I remember." My words are soft. I remember everything with so much goddamn clarity it aches to recall. They say hindsight is twenty-twenty, but I didn't need hindsight with Everly. I already recognized the treasure she was as a drunk twenty-two-year-old under a starlit sky.

She snorts, tapping on the screen of her phone. "I pursued music." She hands me her phone and this time, my mouth drops open, my chin pretty much scraping the floor.

"Holy shit."

4
🎵 everly 🎤

"**Y**ou're famous."

Snatching my phone back, I shrug. "Kind of. I mean, obviously not here." I squint at him through one eye, still miffed that he had no idea that I've become a country singer and songwriter.

He laughs. A real one. One of those belly laughs that expels pent-up emotions until the laughter turns into something else entirely. It's the most real he's been with me since I ran into him, and for a fraction of a second, it's like I see him again. The boy I fell in love with.

"Lee, you were nominated for a fucking Grammy."

"Yeah, but I didn't win."

"Everly," he chides me.

"Aaron." I love playing with him, mainly because his frustration always turns to amusement. At least, it used to.

"How the hell did I not know this?"

"Once again, at the risk of sounding totally conceited, I have no freaking clue. I mean, even I know you went on to take a pretty big leadership role at Anderson Marketing and PR."

"How'd you know that?"

Rolling my eyes, I duck my head, embarrassed that I just threw myself under the bus. "Your company website."

"You stalked me." He points a finger at me, his voice pleased.

"I would hardly call it stalking."

"You were curious about my life?"

"Of course I was curious. After you ended things with us, I just, I wanted to make sure it was worth it."

"If what was worth it?"

"If you, you know, did all the things you planned to do. Work for the family company, have a leadership position, all of it. And you did. I'm proud of you."

Aaron clears his throat, ducking his head.

When he glances back up, his eyes swirl with emotion, regret heavy in the lines of his face. "Everly, I —"

A nurse moves the curtain separating the space from the rest of triage and pops her head inside. "Everly Pierce?"

Seriously? She chooses now to interrupt? When Aaron is finally going to share some insight on why he broke my heart when I was a fresh-faced and eager nineteen-year-old? "That's me." I raise a hand.

"I'm here to take you for X-rays."

Standing slowly, my body aches as my joints click

into place, my muscles stretching. I'm sure my ankle is just sprained, and this entire trip to the hospital is unnecessary.

Aaron stays behind as I'm escorted for my X-ray.

"Try to stay still," the technician, a middle-aged woman instructs, placing the X-ray coat over my chest and stomach.

"Sure." I lie back, my body perfectly still, and close my eyes.

A shudder rolls through me but the memory doesn't give a shit, and *his* face fills my mind the way it always does.

Unbidden and unwelcome.

Pain explodes in my ribs, traveling into my chest and squeezing my heart like a vise until I'm sure it's stopped beating altogether.

Bruises mar my wrists, encircle my neck. Ugly, purple blotches that resemble fingertips too closely to play it off as anything else. Coldness sweeps through me, shutting everything down, numbing out the pain, blocking out the hurt.

"Stay still." The X-ray technician's voice is quiet, soothing, but I hear the sympathy in her tone, read the pity in her eyes.

And realizing that this is how people will see me now shatters me all over again.

"Ms. Pierce. Try to hold still for one more, okay?" The woman pops her head into the room, startling me as my eyes fly open, and I seek out her kind smile, her unknowing eyes, devoid of pity.

"Sure. Sorry about that." My voice sounds scratchy and I clear it, wanting to wash away the dread mixed with fear clinging to my skin like a sticky film.

Shuttering my eyes closed again, I block out the memories of my last trip to the ER. It was a little over a month ago, and yet it seems like it was both years past and seconds earlier.

Time is funny like that, one thing, one scent, or word or smile, can transport you to another place entirely, causing a flood of emotions that are so real in their intensity, yet so misplaced in their timing.

Breathing slowly, in through my nose, hold, out through my mouth, I manage to get through the X-rays and compose myself so that by the time I re-enter the space where Aaron waits for me, I'm in control once more. Still, my heart canters too quickly in my chest, and adrenaline lingers in my bloodstream.

"How were X-rays?"

"I'm pretty sure it's just a sprain. This was unnecessary." I wave a hand to encompass the hospital as I ease back onto the bed and prop up my ankle.

"Why risk it?"

Moving his chair closer to my bedside, he reaches out, his hand steady, his fair skin contrasting against my tanned arm, and fingers the colorful beaded bracelets adorning my wrist. A slight flutter of his fingertips has me sucking in my breath, my eyes latching onto his. Heat and desire travel through his blue eyes, bright and blazing. The space between us shrinks. It's too intimate, too real, too... us.

Ripping my gaze from him, I study the wall over his shoulder. I'm done with heartache and heartbreak. I'm in Scotland to clear my head, to gain perspective, to... reset my life.

"Everly," the doctor sweeps aside the curtain and Aaron stands, moving to the foot of the bed. "I'm Dr. Glenn." He shakes my hand before turning back to the X-rays clasped in his.

"It's not broken, is it?"

"Nope, just a sprain. But you'll have to stay off of it for a few days. Should be healed in two weeks or so if you don't push it."

"That's fine. I know the drill." All too well. Pushing myself to the edge of the bed, I start to stand up when Dr. Glenn's voice stops me.

"I see that." His voice is quiet, but his words are sharp, and dread deadens my momentum, causing me to freeze as embarrassment mixed with panic locks down my limbs.

Shit.

Darting my gaze to Aaron, I take in the confusion rippling over his features, the concern in his eyes as they swing to mine.

How do I explain this? What do I say?

I don't have a chance to smooth over Dr. Glenn's

words because he's not finished. "Would you mind stepping out, Mr....?"

"Anderson. Aaron." Surprise colors Aaron's tone as he crosses his arms over his chest, rocking back on his heels, his gaze swinging from Dr. Glenn to me and back again.

"Right, Mr. Anderson. Could you give us a moment?"

Words, excuses, and lies, sit on the tip of my tongue, ready to extinguish the awkwardness that expands in the room with each passing second. But my throat burns and my nose stings and tears that I'm desperate to conceal threaten to fall, stealing all of my concentration.

"Everly?" Aaron questions, his voice low, his words wrapped in worry.

I shake my head, clearing my thoughts, ignoring the tears, and lock eyes with Dr. Glenn, hoping he understands telepathy and hears the words I can't say.

"I'm fine, Dr. Glenn. Thank you for your time and for the results." Sliding off the bed, I land on my right foot, grateful when Aaron's hand balances me. "But I can manage this just fine."

Dr. Glenn watches me intently for a beat before clearing his throat. "Of course." He pulls a card from his pocket and slips it into my hand, giving my fingers an extra squeeze. "If you have any questions about your ankle, give me a call." His voice is gruff, his eyes darkening with *pity*.

Damn it.

There it is again.

I nod once, avoiding his gaze, hating the concern and compassion and understanding that dwells there. I don't need it. I don't want it. I'm fine. Releasing a shaky breath, I paint on a smile and turn toward Aaron. "Ready?"

"What was that about?" he asks, gesturing between me and the space Dr. Glenn just vacated.

"Oh, you know how doctors are, thorough. Let's get out of here." I hook my fingers around his forearm, as I force myself to move forward.

"I'll stop and get you supplies for the next few days. What do you need?"

Desperate to be done with this experience, back in the safety of my own space, on my own, away from pitying eyes and considerate questions, I don't even think of my words as I blurt them out.

"Oh, it's no worries. I already messaged Dan, and he is going to gather everything I need."

"Dan?"

"My driver."

"You have a driver?"

"I do. In fact, he's here. Thank you for taking me, Aaron. It was very kind of you to take time away from your daughter and The Fringe to sit here with me. I'm all set, though," I ramble as we walk toward the main entrance, and the dread clogging my chest loosens when I spot the black SUV and Dan's hulking frame leaning against it. "I hope I didn't mess up your plans too much, and you can still catch some shows with Livvy."

"It's no problem," Aaron says slowly, his eyebrows bent over his confused eyes. "Give me your phone," he demands, stopping next to the sliding glass doors to outside, to the black SUV, to the air I'm desperate to suck in and cleanse the panic building inside of me.

"What? Why?" I snap, and Aaron's eyebrows dip lower.

Damn it.

"So I can add my number in case you need anything while you're here."

Wincing, I close my eyes and count to five in my head, fishing around in my large hobo bag until my fingers wrap around my phone. Shoving it into his hand, I open my eyes. "Sorry. I just, I'm not feeling well, and I need, I need to go."

Aaron nods, his eyes scanning my face, searching for clues, for insight to explain my behavior.

Forcing my face to fall slack, I give nothing away. It's a skill I learned early on in my career and mastered completely during my last relationship.

Aaron punches in his contact information and drops my cell back into my bag. "Message me if you need anything. I'm serious. Either way, it was good to see you. And I'm real fucking proud of you, Lee."

Emotion clogs my throat, my eyes welling with tears. Nodding, I glance at the floor, at our kissing toes, and bite my bottom lip to rein in the overwhelming emotions unleashed by Aaron's words. At the pride in his tone and the validation I feel. "Thank you."

He nods, shuffling me over to Dan and making sure I'm buckled into the backseat of the SUV before lifting a hand in farewell. "Take care of yourself, Everly."

"You too."

Aaron closes my SUV door, and I lean my head back, closing my eyes as a few stray tears fall, sliding down my cheeks.

If only I knew how to do that.

That's why you're here.

"Home, Ms. Pierce?" Dan asks.

"Please. Thank you, Dan."

Home. Will a place ever feel safe again?

5

aaron

I spend the rest of my weekend consumed with thoughts of Everly.

Why is she really here?

Is she okay?

And what does this mean?

To be honest, it's exhausting, and I need to stay focused on Olivia. She returned home from Paris with a dejection clinging to her like a second skin. Stepping into her bedroom on Sunday night, she's poised in front of her play vanity.

"Hey there, little love."

"Hi Daddy." Livvy's face scrunches adorably as she stares up at me, the tip of her pretend makeup brush hovering in the air. "I have a very important question."

"Yes, little love?"

"Are you going to marry someone new like mummy?" Her voice is quiet as she looks down, suddenly intent on picking a scab on her knee.

Fire.

That's the only word to describe the blinding hate and anger blazing through my body. A wildfire. The kind that spares nothing and no one. Total scorched fucking earth.

"Mummy's marrying?" I swallow thickly, my saliva getting stuck in my throat, so I have to cough around the name I now hate more than any other name in history. "Paul?"

Olivia nods seriously. "She asked me if I'd be the flower girl in her wedding."

Mother fucking hell.

"And I said yes because I'm really fantastic at throwing all the petals. I did such a good job at Sierra and Denver's wedding. Aunt Jenni said I was the best flower girl she's ever seen." Livvy looks back up, seeking confirmation.

"You were perfect."

She nods again. "So, are you?"

"Am I what?"

"Going to marry someone."

"No." The word shoots out of my mouth, resolute and decisive. "I'm always going to be here for you, Olivia. That will never change."

A small smile flickers across Olivia's lips, and some of the worry drains from her face. "Good."

My heart aches for my daughter. Seven years old and already shouldering so many burdens, so many life lessons that I'd never want her to learn in the first place, like the failure of a marriage. Kate and I are setting her up for extensive therapy in her adult life.

Yanking the back of my neck, I sit for a while and watch Olivia play with her makeup set. Her expression is so serious as she applies her eye shadow, her lips forming a pout as she swipes on lipstick. I watch her and feel the space in my chest fill back up with so much anger, I can't dig myself out of it.

She's my life now, the most important person in the world.

And it doesn't matter what I may or may not want; I need to think about my daughter.

When it's bedtime, I read her an extra book and spend time lingering outside her bedroom door, listening to her breathing even out, the slight snore that whistles on her exhales.

When I drop Olivia off at summer camp on Monday morning, I'm relieved that she's eager to attend, some of the melancholy from France melting away. I hope our conversation from last night reminded her just how important she is.

"See you later, Daddy." She waves goodbye, her backpack nearly bigger and heavier than she is, as she rushes to meet her friends.

Blowing out a large exhale, I rock back on my heels, watching my daughter laugh with the girls she knows from school.

"Long summer?" a woman next to me in the drop-off line asks.

"Aye."

"Same. I couldn't wait for camp to start." She flips her sunglasses on top of her head, her eyes zeroing in on the lack of a wedding band on my ring finger.

"I'm sure they'll have fun. Take care," I say abruptly, turning back toward the parking lot. Walking to my car, I note the side eye and long glances from other parents. The women in committed relationships look at me with pity, the single moms with flirtation, and the dads with a hint of judgement.

Jesus. *Is this how it's going to be each morning?*

Insecurities wrap around me like cling wrap as I slide deeper and deeper into a pool of self-doubt.

Could I have saved my marriage with Kate?

How did I miss all the signs?

Was she really so miserable with me that she had to cheat? Was that her way out?

The entire situation depresses me. The shit she pulled, the lying and cheating and lack of mothering to Olivia, stabs at me, but so does the question I abhor: did I cause it? What role did I have in creating a situation that made Kate react the way she did?

Sliding behind the steering wheel, I point my car in the direction of work, desperate for the distraction it provides.

"EVERLY PIERCE?" Finn drops by my office two minutes after I sit behind my desk, about to take my first gulp of coffee. And God, do I need the caffeine this morning.

This weekend was its own kind of torture. I couldn't keep my mind off Everly, of wondering how she was managing with her sprained ankle, of thinking about her and... Dan, the driver.

"Everly Pierce," I confirm, as Finn sits in the chair across from my desk.

"Why didn't you tell me you dated a famous singer?"

"I didn't know she was famous."

"Aaron, she was nominated for a Grammy."

"I recently learned that." I take another gulp of coffee, welcoming the sting burning the roof of my mouth.

My brother rolls his eyes, a grin lifting the corner of his mouth. "Was it strange, seeing her again?"

"Aye."

We sit in silence for several seconds before Finn shakes his head. "So, are you going to ask her out?"

"Ask her out? Of course not."

"Why not?"

"Why would I?" I shoot back, but deep down, the idea intrigues me. Of course it's crossed my mind, but it's stupid. I broke Everly's heart; she told me so herself just two days ago. Plus, I have a daughter. A man with a daughter doesn't date singers who were nominated for a Grammy.

"Because you like her."

"Of course I like her. I dated her."

"It's more than that."

Shaking my head, I down half the contents of my mug. "Do you have anything work-related to discuss?"

"Aaron, you've got to snap out of it. I hate seeing you like this."

"Like what?" I keep my voice even, neutral, but inside my blood is on a slow simmer of anger mixed with self-preservation.

Finn leans back in his seat, his thumb and forefinger plucking at his lower lip. "Mate, you need to pull yourself together," he says finally, leaning forward again. "What Kate did to you was bloody awful. But Aaron, you used to be laidback and funny, sensitive and thoughtful. Now, you're just…" He waves his arm up and down like that explains anything.

"I'm what?"

"Bitter."

I roll my eyes, biting the inside of my cheek, so I don't snap at my brother.

"And it's been six months. You have a daughter. You don't get to still act bitter or jaded or pissed off. You have to show up for her and—"

"I do show up. Every single goddamn day. I—"

"And part of showing up means being present and being the dad that she needs, that she knows. You know, the one who used to let her polish his nails with glitter and have tea parties in forts."

Sighing, I pinch the bridge of my nose. Deep down, I know my brother is right. I haven't been myself since Kate moved to France with her paramour. It wasn't supposed to be like this. Every day, I question, how the hell did I get here? How is *this* my life?

"And then," my brother continues, apparently not finished berating me, "you run into your old girlfriend, the one who left a mark on you, randomly at a music festival. Don't you think that's fate?"

"You're joking, right?"

"I remember how you were when you returned from America. Bloody devastated. Like you were grieving."

"Finn, I was a kid."

"You wouldn't even let us say her name."

"It was my first real breakup."

"She's in Edinburgh. Of all the cities in the world, she's here."

"It's surprising."

"She affects you. I saw the way you looked at her at The Fringe, the way you smiled at her. Aaron, you haven't smiled like that, at anyone, in months."

"Finn, I don't have time for this."

He holds up his hands. "All I'm saying is, you still feel something for her, which is great. Because you need to feel something other than ornery toward someone other than Olivia. So, what's the harm in exploring it?"

"The harm?" I pick up the framed photo of Olivia on

my desk and press it toward Finn. "I'm not interested in exploring anything. I don't want to do casual or meaningless. And I don't want to do committed or marriage. I have a daughter, Finn. A daughter I need to prove to the courts would be better off living in Edinburgh with her father than in Paris with her mother."

Finn sighs. "Aaron, that doesn't mean you need to be single forever."

"It also doesn't mean I should run back to my exgirlfriend."

"Just keep an open mind, yeah?"

"I'll see you at the eleven am meeting." I lift my chin toward the door.

Finn shakes his head at me, like he's disappointed, but he leaves.

Opening my calendar, I glance at the appointments I have today, thankful that I don't have anything pressing until eleven. This summer, I stepped back from my leadership role, decided to take on less mentoring, in order to be more present for Olivia once she returned from Paris. As a result, my schedule is lighter than it used to be.

It's so light that I have time to open the Google search bar and type in "Everly Pierce."

ANGRY.

Irate.

And bloody jealous.

That's what I am.

Because Everly Pierce isn't dating Dan. No, it's worse than that. Much worse.

She's dating Corey Hughes, an executive at the number one country music label in Nashville. The guy's face explodes in my Google search, showing up in every article and in every image. He's a good-looking son of a bitch, but flashy as hell. Designer belts and watches that cost more than my monthly alimony payments. And trust me, that's a lot of money.

But it's the photos of Corey and Everly that bother me the most. Because in them, she's beaming, radiant, literally glowing with happiness. He looks at her like she's the air he breathes. She probably is, the lucky fucker.

So Everly is in a happy, real relationship.

With a man that couldn't be more different from me if he tried. Flashy, rubbing elbows with famous people, jet-setting around the world versus business-casual, rubbing elbows with Finn, playing Uno on a Friday night. *What the hell is the comparison there?*

Nothing.

But then why is Everly here without him?

What did she really mean when she said she was looking for magic?

Doesn't she already have it, own it, keep it bottled up for the nights that she walks down red carpets and takes selfies with other famous people?

Unable to stop myself, I keep clicking, like a lunatic. *A bawbag.*

And then, a photo pops up. A candid. One where Everly didn't realize she was being photographed. She's beautiful, absolutely breathtaking in a sapphire gown, strapless with her signature silver and gold chains and pendants draped around her slender neck. But instead of looking at Corey Hughes like he hung the moon or invented sticky toffee pudding, her eyes are downcast. He has a hand on the small of her back, and her stiffness suggests she doesn't want it there, that she's pulling away from his touch.

Could it have been a lover's quarrel? Of course.

But something about her expression, something about the tension in her shoulders bothers me.

And a lot of something's about Corey Hughes and his claim on Lee causes a jealousy streak like I've never experienced to blaze through me.

THAT NIGHT, after reading Olivia four Katie Morag books, I'm lying in my own bed re-reading a thriller, when a text message dings.

Snatching up my phone, expecting a meme from

Finn or his best friend Roger, surprise rockets through me.

> Unknown: Hey Aaron, it's Everly. I wanted to thank you again for taking me to the hospital on Saturday and pass along my number. I've decided to stay in Edinburgh at least through September. If you'd like to grab a coffee and catch up, let me know.

My heart soars in my chest before crashing and burning.

Rein it in, mate. She has a boyfriend. She's moving back to Nashville. And you have a daughter.

Finn's words from earlier float around in my head. On some level, and as annoying as it is to admit, I know my brother is right. I do need to start living life again, start easing myself out of the depressing pool of failure and anger I've been drowning in.

But Everly, she's dangerous for a man like me. Not because I *want* to be single forever, but because Everly is the one woman in the world who could make me *want* the rest of it. The marriage and the babies and the big house.

And I have Olivia. She's enough for me.

Still, there's no real harm in grabbing a coffee, is there?

Me: Hey Everly. How's the ankle healing? Aye, coffee would be great. Want to meet at The Fray on Leith's Docks Wednesday at one?

I'm pretty sure I don't have a meeting then, and if I do, well, I'll move it.

Everly: Sure! See you then. Goodnight, Aaron.

6

♫ everly 🎤

Nerves zing up and down my spine as I stare at the inside of my closet.

What am I supposed to wear to coffee with Aaron?

Coffee is casual, easygoing. But I feel like a college freshman again about to go on her first date with the sexy, study-abroad student.

Gah!

I don't even know how to do dates anymore. Corey is all I've known for the past four years, and dates with him were more routine than anything else. He laid out the dress I was to wear and left a note with the details for the night, so I would know how to apply my makeup, fix my hair, and most importantly, how to behave appropriately with whatever company we were mixing with.

Once we moved past the beginning stage of our relationship, dates stopped being romantic or sweet; instead, they were a means to an end, one that made him look good, catapulted my career, and earned us both a lot of money. My stomach roils at the thought. In so many

ways, I'm a sell-out and each week I remained with
Corey, a little more of my soul died.

But I'm here now. In Edinburgh. I'm learning to
stand on my own two feet, and there's more magic in
that than in a boyfriend who could tell the difference
between taffeta and chiffon and leave bruises on my arm
in the same sentence.

Pulling out a simple summer dress that skims the top
of my knees and dips low in the back, I slip it over my
head. I slide on strappy silver sandals and fix long,
turquoise teardrop earrings to my ears.

Tossing my wallet and keys into a fringed, brown-
leather crossbody bag, I pick up my phone just as it
rings.

Addison.

"Hey Addi."

"Everly, what the hell? You haven't responded to my
last two emails."

"They both said the same thing."

"So you did read them."

"I read them."

"And?"

Sighing, I sit on the corner of my expertly made bed.
Corey liked the corners tucked a certain way, the
pillows plumped, and old habits die hard. Like, really
hard. "I'm not sure yet."

"Everly Pierce, you are the strongest, bravest
woman I know. You can't give up on your career, on
your livelihood, on yourself, just because that piece of

shit used you as a personal punching bag." Addison's voice is quiet, but her tone is strong, desperate in its intensity to make me believe what she does.

She's the only person who knows my darkest secret, and the fact that she still wants to represent me is a blessing as much as it is a curse. Corey could easily ruin anyone in Nashville, Addison included. I think the only reason he's held off this long is because Addison's family is Old Southern money with a lot of connections. And, he doesn't know that she knows the truth about him. Yet.

"Addi, I—"

"As your manager, I would just like to point out that you've worked too damn hard to give up on the dream that *you* created. Forget whatever bullshit Corey says; it was all *you*," she continues, giving me a dose of tough love that may have been effective if Corey's name wasn't dropped into the sentence.

His name alone causes my skin to sting, like alcohol poured into an open wound.

"And as your friend, I want to tell you that you're too damn good for him, Everly. You're too talented and driven and good for a man like Corey to do what he did and get away with it."

Squeezing my eyes shut tight against the montage of images flickering through my mind at the mention of Corey, I try to regulate my breathing.

Corey and I kissing, taking selfies, sleeping on tour buses, buying a magnet, postcard, and shot glass from every city I performed in, walking the red carpet at the Grammy's.

Corey slapping my cheek, wrapping his thick fingers around my neck, punching me in the stomach.

They blend together, creating a home movie in my mind, a frenzy in my heart, confusing me until I don't know who I am without Corey. For so long, I was defined by him, because he created me. The Nashville-bred singer who wouldn't have been able to cut it on her own. He sculpted me, built me up, perfected me to become Everly Pierce, country artist who sold millions of albums.

Lies. All lies.

"Everly, you still there?"

Sighing, I open my eyes. "I'm here, Addi. Look, we both know I'm going to do the tour. I'm going to do it all, okay? I'm not giving up on myself or my career or any of it. I'm here to re-invent myself, learn who I am independently of *him*, and how to be that woman when I return to Nashville. I need to clear my head, to shore up my defenses, and remind myself how to just be. I just... I need some more time, okay? I'm staying here for another month."

Addison sighs. "You didn't have to run across the world, you know."

"Scotland isn't across the world."

"You could come home. I'd make sure you wouldn't even see him."

I snort. We both know that's impossible. Corey

would somehow detect the moment I landed in Tennessee, and he would sniff me out faster than a bloodhound tracking a missing person.

"Fine, but why Edinburgh?" my friend presses.

"I'm searching for magic. I'll call you soon, Addi." I disconnect the call.

Standing from my bed, I walk over to the floor length mirror hanging on the inside of my closet and smooth down the skirt of my dress. Inhaling, I take in my tanned skin, the warm pink shimmering on the apples of my cheeks, the beach-waves of my hair. No one would ever suspect the scars that line my bones, the wounds that fester in my veins.

And no one else can ever know.

THE AIR SHIFTS the moment he enters The Fray.

Clad in perfectly tailored charcoal suit pants and a light blue collared shirt, the top buttons open, the sleeves rolled up on his forearms, my throat turns to sandpaper, as I drink him in like a desert wanderer.

His light hair is styled simply, his jaw clean shaven. He looks professional but approachable, qualified but likable.

I start to stand from the cafe table I'm seated at, ignoring the twinge of pain in my ankle, when he notices me. The blue of his eyes darken as he drinks me in like an alcoholic about to fall off the wagon. A zing of delight zips down my spine at his obvious appreciation.

My eyes stay glued to his as he walks closer, the air between us intensifying with each step. His jaw tightens, his chest expanding, as he pulls out the chair across from me and sits down.

Pressing his forearms onto the table, he leans forward and brushes a kiss across my cheek. It's simple and sweet and causes butterflies to take flight in my ribcage.

"You smell like coconut," he remarks.

"It's my shampoo."

"It's the same one you used at uni."

I nod.

"I guess some things don't change." The corner of his mouth lifts, a flicker of amusement flashing in his eyes.

"I guess not."

"How's your ankle?"

"Healing. It's a bit sore but feeling much better. In another week or so, I think it will be fine."

"That's good." He leans back in his chair and flags down a server. "I'm glad you messaged me, Lee."

"You are?"

He nods, gesturing for me to order. We both order, and Aaron tacks on two scones before he turns his attention back to me. "Aye. Why do you sound surprised?"

"I don't know. I just, I don't know how to do this with you."

"Because it's been fifteen years?"

"Because when we broke up, I, you, it really affected me."

He sighs, his exhale filled with emotions so heavy they seem to choke both of us. Placing a hand over mine, he shifts closer. "Lee, I'm sorry. Really, I —"

"You don't have to explain." I force myself to say the words because I'm not sure if I can hear the reasons why he broke my heart.

"I want to. When I ended things with you, Lee, I thought I was doing the right thing. You never would have pursued music, your dreams, if you came to Edinburgh with me."

"But you never asked me what I wanted. You just decided for us and —"

"And now you're famous."

"Yes." I whisper, breaking eye contact and slipping my hand from his. "Now I'm famous."

"So your dream came true."

Snorting, I nod, grateful that the server drops off our scones. "Sure."

"I'm happy you're here. To see you."

"Me too, Aar. So, what's been going on?"

He chuckles, taking a sip of his coffee. "Truth?"

"Truth."

"It's been a shitty six months. You ever feel like…" He shakes his head.

"Like what?" I prod, my heart galloping in my chest.

"Like you just went through hell and you're not sure if the worst of it is passing or just beginning?" His eyes connect with mine, a small muscle under his right eye twitching with nerves, with stress.

"It's the eye of the storm."

"What do you mean?"

"You just suffered the high winds, endured the torrential downpour, been battered and bruised and beaten, and now there's this peaceful calmness, this quiet solitude, this moment where you think to yourself, 'is it over?' but you still feel the shadow, the cloud of what's to come. It's the eye of the storm, Aaron. So it's not the beginning or the end... it's just the middle."

His nostrils flare, his eyes brimming with curiosity. "Aye." He admits quietly. "That's how I feel. But how, how the hell do you know that?"

"We all have our stories and our scars," I answer, thanking the server for the cappuccino she places in front of me.

Aaron regards me for a long moment before adding clotted cream to his scone. "Tell me about your life in Nashville."

Relief trickles down the back of my neck that he isn't going to press me for my story. Or my scars. "I guess it's a pretty normal life. I wake up in the morning, head to the studio, spend time at the gym, write in the afternoons, make dinner, sleep." I shrug. "It's not as glamorous or exciting as people think. I get up and go to work, show up, every day, like everyone else."

"Yeah, but you must have tons of friends, an exciting social life?" He asks the question innocently, but his tone holds an edge.

"I work a lot. I don't have a lot of friends. I mostly spend time with Addison, my manager."

"Boyfriend?"

"Nope."

"Lee." He raises his eyebrows.

"Aar."

He sighs, blowing out a deep breath and scrubbing a palm over his chin. "Okay, look, I know I'm going to sound like a stalker but…"

"But?"

"I Googled you."

Snorting, I roll my eyes and take a sip of my cappuccino.

"Corey Hughes?"

7

aaron

I bite down on my tongue the second the question is out of my mouth.

I have no right to ask her about her relationship with Corey and yet, I'm burning with curiosity to know what's between them.

She can never be yours.

But Everly's reaction surprises the hell out of me.

She doesn't push back from the table in anger or glare at me in hurt. Instead, her skin pales, her eyes grow wide and … empty. Her chest rises and falls but the oxygen sucked into her lungs whistles, like she can't gulp it down fast enough.

"Everly?" My hand reaches out, covering hers and she flinches, tugging away, but I hold her hand tightly in my own. "I'm sorry, babe. I shouldn't have asked."

Take it easy, mate. You spooked her.

In fact, that's exactly how Everly looks in this moment. Fucking petrified. "Lee, are you okay?"

Seconds pass like decades before she releases a

stream of air. "I'm fine." She clears her throat, her eyes vacant, her voice dead.

"Bad breakup?"

She snorts. "The worst."

"I'm sorry, love. I had no idea. Every single thing on the internet paints you and Corey like some golden couple but there was nothing about a break-up."

"It's recent."

"Is that why you're here?"

She shrugs, taking a long sip of her cappuccino.

Sighing, I lean back, releasing her hand and taking a bite of my scone.

Everly tries to smile at me across the table, but her eyes fall flat. The sweet innocence she once wore like a cloak has been dulled, jaded.

It bothers me that Corey has had such an effect on her. He must have broken her heart. *Does she miss him? Wish they were still together? Think about him when she slides into bed at night?*

"What about you, Aar? Are you seeing anyone?"

I chuckle past the tightness in my throat. "Absolutely bloody no one. Unless you count Uno games and tea parties dates."

Everly smiles for real this time, some of the tension in her neck and shoulders lessening. "Those sound better than any dates I've been on lately."

"So, you are dating again?"

"Not really. I meant, any dates with Corey."

"You were together long?"

"Four years."

I whistle through my teeth, my hands clenching into fists underneath the table.

An irrational wave of jealousy churns in my stomach and a coldness, like icy fingers, spreads through my veins.

Of course she had serious relationships after you.

Look how upset she is just hearing her ex-boyfriend's name.

Four years together.

You got bloody married!

And yet, as much as I want her to be happy, I bloody hate the thought of her with another man. Any man.

"Did you guys live together?"

She frowns, a line forming between her dipped eyebrows. "We did. Clearly, not anymore. Why all the questions, Aar?"

I smirk, shaking my head. "Just trying to figure out if this guy stole your magic, babe." I polish off the rest of my scone with a breeziness I don't feel and lean forward again, stopping mere inches from her face.

Pausing, I study her closely, note the surprise that widens her eyes. Grin when the green deepens, and her mouth drops open.

She sucks in a sharp breath, her lips parting, her eyes darting to my mouth. "Aar?"

"And because I'm bloody desperate to do this, Lee." Refusing to overthink my actions and what they mean, I wrap my fingers around the silver and gold chains that decorate her neck, tug her closer, and grind my mouth against hers.

It's not sweet or soulful. It's not thoughtful or gentle.

It's raw and demanding and filled with a promise I'm not sure I can deliver on.

But when Everly groans and parts her lips for me to slip my tongue inside her mouth, all my thoughts, anger, and confusion disappear. The only thing I can focus on is kissing the hell out of Everly Pierce.

"What are we doing, Aar?" she whispers a while later.

We're walking Leith's Docks, enjoying the after-noon's warmth, the people watching, each other.

I shake my head, glancing at my watch. "I'm not sure, Lee. I, fuck, I've missed you, Everly. I didn't think it was possible to miss a person who's been missing from my life for so long and yet…here you are."

"Here I am." She snuggles closer into my side and I wrap my arm around her.

"I want you, Lee. More than I can describe. It's absurd and crazy and the worst possible timing and yet, there it is."

She squeezes my bicep, pressing a kiss against my shoulder. "I know what you mean, Aaron. I feel the same way. None of this makes sense and yet, nothing ever made sense when it came to you. I always felt too damn much. But I need you to know that my breakup is recent. I'm not, I'm not in the headspace for a relationship. And my career, it's everything I have right now. I can't just let everything back home go."

"I know that. I'd never ask that of you. I need you to understand that Olivia is my priority, that she'll always come first." I peer down at her, letting her see how serious I am about my daughter.

"As she should."

"So, can we just take this one day at a time?"

"One day at a time. But we have to be honest with each other." Her voice catches and I stop walking, turning to face her and gripping the sides of her neck, my fingers tangling in her hair.

"Promise, babe. Always honest." I swipe a hard kiss across her mouth. "And if we're being honest, I want you more than my next breath, Lee."

She chuckles, reaching up to wrap her hands around my wrists. Stepping into my space, she leans up on her toes and kisses me back. "Prove it, Anderson." Then she steps back, offers me a flirty smirk, and turns on her heel, walking away.

And for the first time in many, many months, I laugh.

The tinier Everly's frame grows in the distance, the harder I laugh until my chest feels like I can inhale deeply again, until the skin on my face doesn't feel so tight, until some of the bitterness built into my blood-stream bleeds out.

Until I feel like a shell of my old self, the real me, someone I haven't caught a glimpse of in a long time.

ON FRIDAY, I send her flowers. It wasn't easy tracking down her address but being a top marketing executive in the city has some perks and some connections. I picked a large bouquet of Black-eyed Susans, the first flowers I ever bought her back when we were college students. At the time, I purchased them because they were cheap. I had no idea they were native to Tennessee and not exactly the type of flowers a guy would bring to a girl on a date.

But now, now they cost a fortune to acquire and send, and I could care less. I just hope that when she sees them, she remembers, and she laughs, the same way she did the night of our first date.

Hours later, she sends me a message.

Everly: Thank you for the flowers. They were super thoughtful of you and I adore them.

Me: You're welcome. Hope they made you laugh.

Everly: They made my day.

> Everly: What are you doing tonight?
> Dinner?

Relieved that Olivia has a sleepover birthday party tonight at her friend's house, I tap out a reply.

> Me: Yes. Pick you up at 8?

> Everly: I'll be waiting.

"Hey." Finn pops his head into my office. "Want to grab a pint or, are you leaving to pick up Liv?"

"No, I have some time. Olivia has a sleepover party, and I'm going to have dinner with Everly."

"Oh?" Finn's eyebrows rise in surprise, a grin pulling his mouth upward.

"It's just dinner."

"It's a step in the right direction."

"I think I liked you better when you were screwing every woman in a skirt. This new you, the one that's committed, sounds too much like a self-help guide."

Finn chuckles. "A self-help guide? Lach's going to love that." He taps out a message to our cousin.

"I can grab a quick pint with you at Reid's Row," I offer, referring to the pub near our office, which is a frequent hangout for Anderson staff during happy hour.

"Aye, let's go."

Shutting down my computer and donning my suit jacket, I follow Finn out of the office, relieved that the work week is over.

"Where's Daisy?" I ask, looking around for her. Daisy started working at Anderson in January, when things between her and my brother were tenuous at best. Since then, she's become an amazing addition to the Anderson team, as well as to our family when Finn finally got his head out of his ass and fell for her.

"Out with her friends tonight."

"She's going to call you steaming." I snort, knowing Daisy's penchant for tequila. And nights out dancing with her friends from the office.

"I'm the designated driver," Finn admits, and I chuckle.

We make the short walk to Reid's and when we enter, the familiar atmosphere of the pub, complete with worn-out wooden floors and long harvest tables, loud chatter and even louder laughter, live music and a swirl of servers, envelops me.

Finn and I head to a table in the back and order two lagers.

"Where are you taking Everly tonight?"

"I have no idea," I admit.

Finn's eyes nearly bug out of his head.

"What?"

"Mate, you really have been out of the dating game a long time."

"Thanks for bolstering my confidence."

"What I mean is, it's Friday night. You can't just show up at a restaurant and expect to be seated. What time are you picking her up?"

"Shit. I didn't even think about that. Eight."

"Hang on." He pulls his phone out of his jacket pocket and types out a message.

"Who are you messaging?"

"Roger. He'll sort something out for you."

Thanking the server for my pint, I take a swig. "I don't even know the hotspots."

"Roger does." Finn clinks his glass against mine and takes a pull.

Roger, Finn's best friend, is a bartender at a trendy restaurant on Leith's Docks. He tends to know the hottest restaurants, how to snag a reservation, and all news related to the growing F&B scene in Edinburgh.

Moments later, Finn's phone chimes with a message. "You're taking her to Felipe's on the Docks. Reservation for eight-thirty. It's Portuguese and has amazing reviews. Daisy's been dying to try it."

"Thanks, Finn," I say seriously, suddenly nervous for tonight.

"Just try to have a good time. Be yourself."

I raise my eyebrows at my brother. "Are you trying to give me dating advice?"

"I *am* giving you dating advice. Aar, you don't need to marry this woman but—"

"Well, that's a relief. Since I'm never marrying again."

"But you do need to get out there. I'm relieved you're going out, even if it is with an ex-girlfriend. The past few months," Finn whistles low, "you've been a fucking shadow. I'm not saying Everly is going to fix everything for you, but I think she'll help you gain some perspective from everything that happened with Kate. You need this, Aaron. So go out and have fun and for once, just enjoy yourself."

"Aye," I agree quietly, drinking my pint. I do need this.

I need a bit of my own magic to restart my life.

8

🎵 everly 🎤

Wiping my sweaty palms on the front of my dress, I hate how nervous I am. I shouldn't be nervous around Aaron; I never was before. But this, dating, is new to me. And it leaves a sour taste in my mouth.

What if he hates my dress?

What if he doesn't like the way I fix my hair?

Or I say the wrong thing?

Gah!

Aaron isn't Corey.

But Corey wasn't always like Corey, either. In the beginning, he was thoughtful and attentive, considerate and charming. It wasn't until my career started to outshine his that the name calling started, followed by the insults, and then the accusations. His type of abuse didn't happen overnight, but slowly, the way snow melts after a winter freeze. By the time his fists got involved, my self-esteem was shredded. I questioned myself more than I questioned him. Some days, I still do.

Staring at my reflection, I force myself to say the

words my therapist Nicole taught me, "You are strong. You are independent. You are worthy."

Exhaling, I grab my clutch off my dresser and walk into my kitchen when a knock sounds on the door.

"Hey." I pull the front door open, grinning at Dan.

"Heading out?"

"Yes, I have a date." I twirl before stepping back so Dan can enter the foyer.

"With that guy from the hospital?"

"Aaron."

"Yeah. Him?"

I nod.

"Do you need a ride?" he asks, glancing at his watch.

"Nope, he's picking me up. You can take the rest of the night off."

He glances at me for a moment so long, his stare turns into a glare.

I shiver under his harsh gaze, my stomach dropping. Taking a step back, panic unfurls in my stomach and my ears ring.

What the hell is happening?

Dan blinks. "Thanks, boss. I will."

I nod, clutching the doorframe.

It's fine. You're fine.

You're just nervous.

Dan, while having glowing recommendations, isn't known for his friendliness but rather his prowess to protect.

"Be careful, Everly. Call if you need me." He nods once before stepping back into the hallway.

Closing the door behind him, I grip the doorknob and frown at his word choice. I'm sure he just meant for me to be careful going out in Edinburgh, but his tone seemed serious, borderline sinister.

Glancing down at my phone, I breathe out a long exhale when I read Aaron's message.

> Aaron: I'm here.

I have a date. I can do this. I'm strong and independent and worthy.

I'm badass.

Meh, at least I'm trying to be.

Locking the door behind me, I bound down the steps toward Aaron's car.

He's leaning against it, his ankles crossed casually, his arms folded against his chest. But his expression, the way he looks at me, causes an extra bounce in my step.

Aaron's eyes light up, and it warms me from the inside out.

It smooths some of my jagged edges and causes a swell of hope to rise in my chest, shimmering like a sprinkle of stardust. This is exactly what I need. A chance to dip my toe back in the dating pool with someone I trust. Someone safe.

"You look beautiful, Lee." He kisses my cheek, the spice of his cologne wrapping around me.

"Thank you."

"I mean it." He pauses, his fingertips tracing the back of my hand. "You're glowing."

I shiver under his praise, internally rolling my eyes at myself. *You're here to stand on your own two feet, not melt into a puddle at every little compliment.* "Thanks."

Sliding into the passenger seat, Aaron closes the door behind me. Once he's settled behind the steering wheel and we're driving on the main road, he glances at me from the corner of his eye.

"How do you feel about Portuguese for dinner?"

"I have no idea what that entails."

Aaron chuckles. "Think seafood."

"Oh, no. I'm allergic."

Aaron's foot slams on the break, and I jerk forward, the seatbelt cutting into my chest.

"Since when?" he asks, panic breaking out on his face.

Snorting, I can't contain the peals of laughter that erupt from me. "I'm just kidding. Oh my God, you should see your face."

The pallor of Aaron's face dims as color floods his cheeks. He groans. "You are seriously the worst."

"I love seafood."

"I remember." He frowns, turning his attention back to the road.

"Don't be mad. I'm just messing with you." I back-track. *Did I push him too far? Is he angry?* "That was stupid of me. I shouldn't have assumed you would laugh. I'm so dumb to—"

"Hey." Aaron places a hand on my thigh and squeezes lightly. "It's fine. Don't say that about yourself. I overreacted."

I shake my head, panic shimmering along the edges of my line of sight. "I'm sorry."

"Everly, seriously, it's fine. I'm just nervous for tonight."

"You are?"

Aaron nods, removing his hand from my thigh and tugging on the back of his neck. "I haven't really dated since, well, it's been a really long time."

"For me, too."

He glances over, curiosity stamped onto his expression. "Why did you and Corey break up?"

I shrug, glancing out the window. "We didn't see eye to eye."

"About what?"

Everything. "Our futures. We just—we want different things."

"When did you break up?"

"You already asked me that. It wasn't too long ago."

Aaron chuckles. "You're holding your cards close to your chest."

I smirk at him over my shoulder before returning my gaze to the window. "About ten weeks ago. Afterwards, well, it's why I originally came to Scotland. Needed a break, a fresh perspective."

"Ten weeks," Aaron repeats, his voice low.

"Ten weeks."

"How's your new outlook working out for you?"

This time, I turn to face him. "I'd say pretty great, wouldn't you?"

He laughs, nodding, but a shadow flickers over his face, reminding me this is temporary.

That Aaron and I can never work.

I'm not ready for real. I'm not ready for much of anything although having dinner with Aaron feels like a win. Nicole will be proud of my progress during our weekly call session.

Arriving at the restaurant, Aaron parks his car and takes my hand as we walk toward Felipe's. Lacing our fingers together, I'm hyperaware of every twitch of his fingers, each gentle squeeze he presses into my palm. When he looks down at me, he winks, his face open.

My body automatically turns toward him, on cruise control. I don't have to think when I'm around Aaron; I naturally respond and react to every move he makes. We did this dance once before, and our bodies seem to remember, even if our hearts prefer to forget certain parts.

The atmosphere inside Felipe's is warm and inviting, soft candlelight, colorful mosaic tiles, and the cheerful din of couples and families and friends enjoying a meal. Sitting down at a table set for two, I pick up my menu and glance over the top at Aaron, not surprised to find him staring at me.

"We've come a long way from devouring ribs at Gussie's BBQ, haven't we?" I ask, referencing a BBQ place we frequented in college.

Aaron chuckles. "I guess so, but those were good times."

"The best times," I agree, scanning the menu.

"How do you feel about wine?"

"It's one of my food groups."

"Good. Portuguese wine is really good and undervalued."

"Order away."

When the server stops by our table, Aaron orders a bottle of red wine and sparkling water. The candle flickers between us, casting soft shadows over Aaron's face. His presence seems to grow each time I see him, until he's filling all the aching spaces inside of me, all the gaping holes Corey created with his hateful words and rampant distrust.

Feeling nervous under Aaron's scrutiny—what if he finds me lacking?—I'm grateful for the glass of wine that is soon placed in my hand.

"To tonight." I gesture with my glass toward Aaron.

"To you," he responds, his eyes fixed on mine, the heat flickering in their blue depths heady, captivating my attention and causing my skin to tingle with awareness.

Sipping the wine slowly, the bold flavor of a full-bodied grape bursts on my tongue. "It's good."

"Aye."

"Do you drink wine often?"

"No, I'm more of a lager or Scotch guy."

"And whiskey?"

"Only with you, Lee."

I grin at his words, leaning closer to him over the table. "So, tell me, what have you been up to these past fifteen years?"

Aaron shakes his head. "Nothing as exciting as your life."

"I don't know. It seems like life would be very colorful with a kid like Livvy."

Aaron's laughter is unexpected, and he nods. "It is. She's a great kid. A little too mature for her age but that's my fault. She's always around adults since she's the only kid in the family, well, not counting Sierra's newborn."

"Does she have a lot of friends?"

"A few. I should probably invite them over for a play date. Lately, Livvy's been going to all of her friends' houses to play, but we haven't had anyone over to our place." His brows furrow, as if he's realizing something important. "Kate always handled the play dates. I don't even know how to do that."

"You could ask Olivia which friends she would like to invite over and go from there."

"Aye, that's true," he agrees, blowing out an exhale. "It's a lot, you know, becoming a single parent overnight. But I want Olivia with me for the school year now that Kate's living abroad."

"That makes sense. Do you think Kate will agree?"

Aaron nods, pinching the skin next to his eye. "Aye, that's another problem. I think she will agree, and I keep wondering how Livvy will feel about that. Most mums would say screw Paul and France and stayed in Edinburgh for their kids, but for Kate to choose her new life over what's best for Olivia concerns me. I mean, what mums do that?"

I shrug. "The ones who know they can't provide as well as the other parent."

"I guess so. Honestly, I've been so angry lately, so unlike myself, I think I'm looking for reasons to be mad."

"That makes sense. It's hard, moving on, moving past what you once thought of as your entire world. You're doing an amazing job with her." I cover his hand with mine, and he flips his hand over, palm up, until he can thread my fingers with his.

"Thank you. She's the best thing in my life." He hesitates, squeezing my hand. "I'm happy you're here, Lee. I really am. I want to spend time with you. But I need you to understand that Olivia is my only priority right now."

His words sting, even though they shouldn't. I can't seriously date right now, either; I have priorities. Like learning how to be on my own, look out for myself. Like my upcoming tour.

"I get that." I keep my voice steady, my expression playful. I've mastered the art of casual over the years, and I'm relieved I can rely on it now. "I'm not in a place where I can do serious, either."

Aaron frowns. "Because of your ex?"

"Yes," I sigh, "Corey changed the game for me."

Aaron's expression darkens, but he doesn't say anything.

I think we're both a little relieved when our entrees arrive.

9

aaron

I hate Corey Hughes.

It's the only thing I can think as I cut into my fish fillet and take a large bite, barely appreciating the delicious flavors exploding in my mouth because I'm too focused on Everly's forlorn expression when she says her ex's name.

Bloody Corey Hughes.

Shoveling a forkful of rice into my mouth, I calm the irrational surge of jealousy I feel toward Everly. I'm frustrated, angry even, that she's so hung-up on a guy who, by the looks of it, waxes his eyebrows.

"This is delicious," Everly comments on her entree, taking delicate forkfuls and chewing slowly, enjoying her meal like a normal person.

For some reason, this riles me up even more. How can she enjoy her food when I'm reacting like a caveman to the fact that she's still affected by her breakup after dating Corey for years? Of course it's still bothering her; it happened ten weeks ago.

Kate and I divorced half a year ago, and I still want to throw something when I think about her.

"Aye," I answer, taking a large gulp of my wine.

"How's work? Tell me about Anderson."

Checking my anger at her innocuous question, I start to calm down, launching into an explanation about my work responsibilities. "But the part I love best is the mentoring, even though I recently cut back to have more time with Liv."

"Really?" Everly's eyebrows rise. "I mean, I can totally see that about you. You've always been more of a leader than a follower."

"I actually mentored Daisy earlier this year when she started at Anderson."

"Oh, my God. Is that how she and your brother met?" Everly leans closer, her smile genuine.

"No, it's complicated. Daisy is my cousin Sierra's best friend. My whole family has known her for years. But last Christmas, Finn was stranded Stateside after a snow storm, so he joined Sierra and her now-husband Denver for Christmas, and I don't know, something happened between him and Daisy. She had already accepted her position at Anderson. Needless to say, it was a bit stressful for Finn when she started working at the family company."

"I bet." Everly laughs. "But they managed to work it out."

"Aye." I chew another bite thoughtfully. "It took them long enough to figure their shit out."

"Sometimes, it's not so obvious to the people actually falling that they're falling."

I bite the inside of my mouth to keep from smiling at her. I knew I was falling for Everly at twenty-two. And I know if I'm not careful, I could fall for her now, too.

But things are different this time. We're not naive, college kids, with bright ideas about even brighter futures. This time around, I'm a father with responsibilities and obligations I have to uphold. And Everly is a broken-hearted superstar, with a thriving career on the other side of the Atlantic.

Still, as we gradually proceed to order rice pudding and creme caramel for dessert, I can't help but wonder what our future would look like if things were different.

If I could claim Everly's heart again.

"Come home with me," I whisper into her hair, as we walk back to my car. Rubbing my thumb over the feather tattooed between her thumb and wrist, I hold my breath in my lungs waiting for her response.

"What about Olivia?"

"She's at a friend's slumber party."

"Are you sure?" She tilts her head toward me, her eyes studying me in the moonlight.

"That I want you? I've never been more certain about anything in my life."

Everly smiles at my words. I'm struck by how unbelievably beautiful she is, her green eyes dazzling, brimming with a soulful sincerity that only she possesses. "Okay."

"Okay." I squeeze her hand one last time before she slips into my car.

The drive back to my flat is quiet, both of us lost in our thoughts. But it's a comfortable silence, one that speaks to a shared history, a past that was intense in its depth. I once loved Everly Pierce with every fiber in my being and sitting in my car with her next to me reminds me just how easily I could again.

Women like Everly, they imprint on your heart, ruining you for every woman that comes after them. Even wives, which I'll admit is awful. I'm not sure I even realized it until this moment, but I don't think I ever felt the same degree of feelings for Kate that I felt for Everly. The passion was overwhelming, the yearning constant. Even now, after fifteen years, I want her more than my next breath, and by the time I park by my flat, my hands are clenched into fists, and I'm needy for her touch.

When her gaze swings to mine, whatever she reads in my eyes causes her own to flare with desire, heat with a lust I'm desperate for her to act on.

She stumbles on the way to my flat, and I steady her as her laughter rings out around us. She's flushed from the wine, her eyes bright, her body relaxed. The silver and gold chains around her neck shimmer under the fluorescent lights of the hallway, and the messy waves of her hair brush over her shoulders.

She's so damn effortless, so alluring. I can't think clearly. All I know is I need to have her, to pin her against the nearest surface and step into her until her warmth melts the ice in my heart, until her sweetness quells the fury in my blood.

Everly could shatter and save me. And tonight, I want both.

Swinging the door to my flat open, I wait for her to enter before kicking the door closed and leaning back against it, my arms folding across my chest.

Everly spins to face me, a grin spreading across her lips until she bites the corner of her mouth, teasing and tempting. She continues to back away until she's across the room, leaning against my dining table. Her hands hook below the table top as she leans her weight against it, her eyes trained on mine.

I groan. "Damn it, Everly."

She reaches up, slipping the straps of her simple sundress over her shoulders. The slinky material slides down her frame slowly. With each inch of skin revealed, my breathing intensifies, my fingers itchy to reach out and touch her. To feel the smooth silk of her skin, to breathe in the sweet coconut of her hair, to feel the heat of her mouth against mine.

Her dress pools at her feet, and she steps out of it, kicking it behind her underneath the table. Slipping out of her flats, she kicks them away too. Clad in a lacy pair of underwear, topless, she shoots me a playful grin.

"Fuck, Everly." I take a step closer. "What are you doing to me?"

"Like what you see?" she taunts, hoisting herself onto the table.

"Do you always do this little striptease number?" I demand, desperate for the answer to be no.

"Never."

"Why me?" I ask, stepping in between her thighs, my hands braced on either side of her hips.

"Because you're the only man to ever really see me," she whispers, her eyes solemn, all playfulness gone.

Dipping my head, I capture her lips with mine.

Her kiss rips through me, an electric current that zaps and zings everything in its wake. My blood is on fire as I lay her back on the dining room table. Her skin shimmers in the moonlight poring through the floor-to-ceiling windows from the living room. The nightscape of the city washes us in a pale glow as I cover Everly's body with mine.

Her moans are sweet little mewls of satisfaction, her eyes fluttering closed. Pressing a kiss to each eyelid, I feel the curve of her smile against my chin.

"I missed you, Aaron. Being with you, it's the closest I've ever felt to home." Her voice is a whisper, a confession that feels safe in the darkness.

"Missed you more," I manage, the blood thrumming

in my temples, a roar of pent-up fervor, of years of wanting and yearning, spilling out of me like ink, marking her skin and hopefully branding her heart.

I work her over slowly, paying attention to the sounds falling from her lips, the way her body clenches and shudders under my touch.

My fingers skim over a series of raised bumps near her hip and I frown, pausing to trace the scars with my thumb. I begin to pull away, questions forming in my mind. "Lee? What hap—"

"Please." Her fingers dig into my shoulders, pulling me closer, erasing any space that exists between us. She places an open-mouthed kiss at the base of my throat, her tongue flicking out and I groan, all questions vanishing.

Rocking into her, the simmer between us flares into a blaze that consumes me until all I can focus on is her, this moment.

Us.

"HERE." I hand Everly a glass of wine. She's reclined against the pillows near my headboard, dressed only in my button-down, the cuffs rolled back. The beach waves of her hair are tangled from my fingers, her lips swollen from my kiss. She's positively bewitching, even more so because she doesn't realize it.

She doesn't comprehend just how much she captivates me, her intellect holding me prisoner, her body demanding that I surrender. Everything about Everly could force me to wave a white flag to all my own hang-ups: the distance, my status as a dad, my failure in my marriage, all of it.

Could it be possible? Could Everly and I have a future together?

It's not like we're getting married or anything rash; we could just date, explore our attraction, the intense pull between us.

Don't we owe that to ourselves?

"What are you thinking about so seriously?" she asks, scrunching her eyebrows at me.

"You."

A wicked smile curves her lips. "What about me?"

"Everything about you. You're bewitching."

She tosses her head back and laughs, the column of her neck on full display. "That's rich coming from you. You may be the only person who could render me speechless. I can't even form thoughts, never mind words, when your hands are on me."

"That's a very good thing, Lee. Because I don't want you thinking about anything but my hands."

She grins, taking a sip of her wine. "What else are you thinking?"

"Things about us."

She raises her eyebrows, dipping her chin for me to continue.

"I know it's all complicated, even more so now than it was back then. But I don't want to give up on us again, Lee. Not without really trying. I have no idea what that looks like, but I want to give things a chance. This time around, I want to make it work."

The sage in her eyes expands, stamping out the other shades of green, until two pools of springtime shimmer at me. She gives a slow nod. "I want that, too. More than anything. But Aaron, I know I've already said this, but I need you need to understand that I'm not giving up my career. I'm not going to—"

"I would never ask you to. Ever. Let's just take it one day at a time. I need to make sure Olivia is comfortable with everything, too. I won't jeopardize my daughter's well-being, her mental health, her happiness, anything." I stare at Everly to make sure she understands exactly what I'm saying. As much as I care about her, Olivia will always come first.

"I would expect nothing less of you."

Taking the wine glass from her hand, I set it on the bedside table and brush my nose against hers. "Then it's settled."

Tilting her face up, she presses her lips to mine, sealing the deal.

And I take my first full breath in more than a year.

10

♫ everly 🎤

I'm dancing through my life like it's a Broadway musical.

Just two weeks of dating Aaron has dulled months of agony with Corey.

A handful of ice cream parties with Olivia has stamped out the worry that used to plague me for eating a dessert.

Being pulled into Aaron and Olivia's lives is a salve to the pain and hurt I've carried around for far too long.

For the first time in so, so long, I feel full, bursting with energy and confidence and a happiness that scares me in its intensity. I've forgotten what fulfillment, what peace, feels like, how it nourishes the soul and calms the mind.

In short, I feel fan-fucking-tastic.

Giving Dan the day off, I leave the posh, high-fashion shops surrounding my apartment and head to The West End, an eclectic enclave of independently owned shops mixed with pubs and restaurants. Colorful storefronts, cobble stoned streets, and Georgian Architecture greet me as I dive headfirst into the bustling shopping and revelry occurring in this part of town.

Heading down William Street, the cool breeze of September ruffles my hair and speaks to the changing season, but the sky is bright blue, blessing the day with good weather. Popping into a jewelry boutique showcasing pieces by local designers, I scan the beautiful necklaces and earrings with the sudden urge to purchase something for myself.

Something to mark today so that in the future, wherever I am and whatever I'm doing, I can catch a glimpse of my bauble and recall this moment, this feeling. I'll remember what it felt like to feel whole again.

"May I help you?" a salesclerk asks.

I point to a simple necklace, a rose-gold plated seashell.

The salesclerk places it in my hand, and I fasten the necklace around my neck, stooping to see how it looks in a mirror. The shell nestles in the hollow of my throat, simple but striking, delicate yet durable.

"I'll take it," I decide. Passing over my credit card, I add, "I'll wear it out."

Stepping back onto William Street, I breathe in the sunshine, the charge in the air, the day.

Seashells symbolize rebirth, resurrection, and right now, I grasp both with open hands, an open mind, and most importantly, an open heart.

I spend the morning popping in and out of boutiques. I buy myself a fantastic journal with a crown embossed on the front and declare it as a space to write down what I'm most grateful for each day. It's time I start counting my blessings. I also purchase new stationary. And then, just because I want to, I buy myself the most beautiful bouquet of flowers. Overflowing with greenery and bold colors, excitement hums through me as I picture the pop of color the floral arrangement will bring to my simple apartment.

Stepping back onto the street, I breathe in the architecture, soak in the delicious Scottish accents, and let the perfect atmosphere fill me with appreciation for this moment in my life.

Sure, things haven't been easy, but my experiences brought me to right now. To this. And this, this is about as good as it gets. Breathing in the new, letting go of the old, things appear clearer, sharper. Both literally and figuratively. This morning, I stop to admire the incredible architecture of The West End, pausing to appreciate The Georgian House, deciding to step inside on a whim and peruse the artwork, the fashionable dressing garments of the late eighteenth century, and the furnishings of the period.

About halfway through my tour, my stomach grumbles, and I laugh at myself, pressing my hand to my abdomen. Wrapping up my visit, I treat myself to lunch and a glass of wine. Taking my first sip of a crisp Pinot Grigio in a bustling restaurant, my phone rings.

"Addison Grace," I answer, grinning.

"Everly? Is that you?"

I laugh. "Yes, why?"

"You sound… happy. Like, I don't even know who you are."

"I am happy."

"Uh-oh." Her tone is teasing, and I know she is grinning, but still an edge of hesitancy laces her words.

"What uh-oh? You're supposed to be happy that I'm happy."

"I am. Truly, Everly, it's incredible to hear some light in your voice after so much dreadful dark."

"But?"

"But, I have a feeling your good vibes are because of a certain ex-boyfriend?"

Rolling my eyes, I sigh. "Yes, fine, part of it is because of Aaron, but part of it is also because of me. I'm, I don't know, healing. Embracing the day. Seizing the moment."

"Carpe diem, babe. But don't forget that you're leaving soon. You have a life and a career—one that is still managing to soar despite your recent neglect—in Nashville. You swore you'd never give a man power over your life again."

"Having phenomenal sex on a dining room table and in the shower and pressed against floor-to-ceiling windows overlooking the city isn't giving away my power. It's creating it and using it to fuel me with good energy," I snap back.

Silence.

One second, two seconds, three… and then, a burst of laughter.

"Oh my God!" my best friend exclaims. "Good for you, Everly. Jesus, I've been waiting for you to bang someone for years now."

"What?"

"This is good. I take back everything I said. Go forth and get naked as much as you can with your Scottish lover."

Taking another gulp of my wine, I try to navigate the confusion that this conversation is causing. "Um, Addi, what are you talking about? You're confusing the hell out of me."

"Ev, sex is good. It's an important step to you moving on from cockless Corey."

I snort at Addison's nickname for Corey, especially now that there isn't any chance of him overhearing her. For so long, her casual use of the nickname caused anxiety to wash over me like a tsunami. What if Corey overheard her? What if someone told him in jest? What if, what it, what if…? But now, finally, I can embrace my freedom and laugh along with her because the truth is Corey is fucking cockless. Any man who treats a woman the way he treated me is clearly overcompensating for… well, everything.

"I'm proud of you. This is a massive improvement. But don't go getting attached or falling in love or anything dumb. You need to stay in control of your ship, chart your own course, steer your own destiny, blah,

blah, whatever the analogy is. You get my drift?" Addison continues.

"I feel ya, babe. But today, I'm happy. I'm zen. I'm in a really good place. So, let me have today. In fact, I'm drinking a delicious Pinot Grigio as we speak." I take another sip, closing my eyes.

"All right, you enjoy your wine. I was just calling to check in on you, and you've passed with flying colors."

"I've always been an overachiever."

"I know, which is why your overachieving ass needs to get back to Nashville in one more month. At the latest." Addison's tone is stern, adding weight to the reality that I can't hide from my life forever. "Everly?"

"I heard you. One month."

"Enjoy your wine." She clicks off.

Opening my eyes, I study the delicious salad I ordered and lift my fork. But Addison's reminder has muddled my appetite. One month.

I'm happy. I'm zen. I'm in a good place.

And damn, I really wanted it to last more than one measly month.

DENIAL.

It's clearly something I excel at. It's an incredible tool for blocking out the present, reality, what I know to be true, and convincing myself of something else entirely.

I've done it for years with Corey.

He loves me. He wants the best for me. He means well.

It's my fault. I caused this. I don't understand him.

Clearly, it's bullshit.

But now, I'm wading into that pool all over again.

I can do casual. It's just sex (ha!). I don't need more.

But damn, do I want more. I want everything with Aaron; I always have.

My time here has been infused with a lightness, one that colors my outlook. I can see myself here, calling this place home, embracing Aaron and Olivia as my family. An old dance, one I remember the steps to but haven't done in a long time, spins around me like a web, wrapping me up in a bliss I don't want to sacrifice again.

Everything between Aaron and me is natural, organic, and easy. Too easy. The type of easy that has my qualms rising and doubts creeping in. Because deep down I know, better than most, that if something seems too good to be true, it is. Things like this never last, and eventually my past will find me.

I haven't heard from Corey once in the two months I've been in Scotland. The more time that passes has me suspended between a relief that maybe he has moved on and a fear that he's plotting something that will blind-side me when it occurs.

I know I have to return to Nashville to start my tour. Addison's reminder hangs like a rain cloud, but I know how to hold an umbrella. I swore I would never compromise my career for a man again. It's the one thing I have that is mine alone. Music is my passion, and touring pays my bills. I can't sacrifice my passion or my financial independence for any man, not even one as incredible as Aaron Anderson.

But right now, in the moments where I detect Aaron's cologne clinging to my bedsheets or spot the coffee he likes in a shop, I know it's hopeless. That I won't be able to walk away until the very end, until I'm forced to let go by forces greater than me, him, us. Whether my heart shatters a second time is irrelevant. Whether I'm left so broken I'll never fly again isn't important.

Because all I can see when I look at Aaron is respect and sincerity. He views me the way I want to, the way I strive to. He sees the real me, the strong me, the resilient me I've been slowly rebuilding. And I can't let her go, not when I'm finally healing.

So I stay, and I fall harder, and I enjoy every second.

Knowing that when the end comes, it will obliterate me.

When he pops by my apartment on Tuesday evening with a brown paper bag filled with takeout, I fling the door wide open and kiss him with reckless abandon.

"How was your day?" he asks, as he steps inside my

apartment and places the takeout bags on my kitchen island.

"Pretty great. I started working on a new song. Two songs, actually. It was really productive. I love writing at all the coffee shops or sitting outside and enjoying the beginning of autumn. It's not this cold yet back home, and I'm sure I'm going to miss it."

Even though his back is still to me, I don't miss the way his body tenses. The muscles in his back clench, his neck stiffening in response to my words.

He turns, leaning his lower back against the kitchen island. "Are you going back soon?"

"In a month or so." Out of habit, I shuffle back a step.

Aaron takes a step toward me, his hand outstretched.

I retreat. Two steps. Three steps.

Aaron's eyebrows bend, his mouth flattening. "Why are you backing away?" His tone is calm, gentle even, and the breath I didn't realize I was holding leaks out.

"Are you mad?" I ask.

"Mad? That you're going on tour for your incredible album?" He grins, shaking his head. "Of course I'm not mad, Lee. I'm so bloody proud of you it isn't even funny." He steps closer now, and for the first time, I don't back away.

Once he's near enough to lace my fingers through his, he wraps our joined hands around his waist until I'm flush against his chest. Dropping a kiss to the top of my head, he whispers, "But I'm definitely going to miss you this time around."

I smile against the fabric of his lightweight sweater. "You didn't miss me the first time?"

Since my ear is pressed against his chest, I hear the rumble of his chuckle as it reverberates through his body. "The first time, I mourned you. I never thought I'd see you again. That our paths would cross, that this" —I glance up to find him peering down at me—"would ever happen."

"And now?"

"Now, I'll miss you properly. Because I know I'll see you again, Everly. Whatever this is between us, we can call it anything we want, but the only thing I know for sure is that it's not goodbye. It will never be goodbye when it comes to you."

Reaching up on my tippy toes, I place my lips against Aaron's and kiss him hard, with purpose and intent, and a million words I want to say but don't know how.

Denial be damned.

THURSDAY, September 14, 3:41PM

Aaron: Hi love, hope you're having the best day. Are you free on Friday night? Come to family dinner at my Aunt Jenni's?

Me: Hey you. I'd love to, thanks. What can I bring?

Aaron: Just yourself. I'll pick you up at 6PM.

Me: I'll be waiting.

Thursday, September 14, 7:11PM

Aaron: Miss you.

Me: One more day.

Aaron: What are you doing tonight?

Me: Grabbing a quick bite with Dan and then working. You?

Aaron: When can I hear your new song? Having a tea party with Livvy and getting my nails done. She wants to know if you'll do her toes next time you're here.

Me: (laughing face emoji) Send a photo! As soon as the song is completed, you can hear it. Don't forget—pinkies up. And, I'd love to do pedicures with my fave girl.

Aaron: (kissing face emoji) Chat later, love.

Thursday, September 14, 10:22 PM

Me: How was the tea party?

Aaron: (image of tea party, Aaron dressed up in purple boa, yellow star-shaped sunglasses, a blue teacup in hand)

Me: Love this!

Aaron: We had fun. How was your song writing?

Me: Productive.

Aaron: Almost done?

Me: Desperate to hear it?

Aaron: You have no idea. But more desperate to see you.

Me: Tomorrow. Sweet dreams, Aar.

Aaron: Night, Lee.

11

aaron

"You okay there, boss man?" Daisy asks, popping into my office and taking the chair opposite my desk.

"Hm? Yeah, I'm fine." I look up from my email. "What are you up to?"

She holds up a mug of coffee, placing it next to my keyboard. Next, she waves a blue folder and adds it to a pile on my desk. "For the Jones account. Here are some concept mock-ups. Cameron has a ton of great ideas he wants to go over, too. Can we all meet early next week?"

I nod, pulling up my calendar. "Tuesday around ten?"

"Perfect."

"Okay. I'll send you and Cameron meeting invites. Thanks for the coffee."

A few seconds tick by as Daisy continues to stare at me.

"Can I help you with something, Dais?" I grin at her. Daisy has been with Anderson for nearly ten months now, and in such a short amount of time, she's become my point person on several projects. With her attention to detail, creative thinking, and engaging personality, we work really well together. Better than Finn and I ever did.

"You're seriously not going to tell me?"

"Tell you what?"

"About you and Everly." She leans forward in her chair, her eyes widening. "I had to hear about her from Livvy. Why else would I bring you coffee?"

"You know, that did catch me by surprise, but I didn't want to make a big deal out of it in hopes that you would continue to do so."

"Spill it, Aaron."

"We used to date."

"Something I can't believe you withheld from me. You do know I hardcore fan-girl over her, right?"

"Dais, I didn't withhold anything. I didn't know she became a singer."

Daisy shakes her head at me, disappointment written all over her expression. "Sometimes, I feel like I don't even know you."

"Okay, fan-girl. Name one of her songs."

"'Mending Broken.' It's her new single. It's bomb. You should listen to it."

"I will. And because you're the best, I'll fill you in on some news."

"I'm listening." Daisy leans closer.

"Everly is coming to dinner tonight."

"Shut up!" Daisy claps her hands together, her face beaming. "You're serious? You're not just pranking me? Because I was super disappointed that Finn met her at The Fringe and I didn't. And, I will point out, that I was the only one invested in making sure Livvy saw a children's show, so it was pretty messed up that everyone except me met Everly. Olivia is practically replacing me with her, with all this chat about ice cream dates and pedicures."

"Tonight is your chance, Dais."

"You have officially redeemed yourself."

"I didn't even realize I was on your shit list."

"It was a brief moment in time. Now that you've invited my idol to dinner, you're forgiven."

"Thank God, I was wondering how I was going to get through the rest of the day."

"Shut it. I'll see you at dinner tonight."

I nod, picking up the coffee mug and taking a sip. "Daisy, this is cold."

She shrugs, her hand hovering on the door handle. "I've gotten what I came for, Aaron. The coffee's on you." She steps out, closing the door after her, and I laugh.

Looking back at my computer screen, I pull up YouTube and type in "Mending Broken." The official video pops up and I click play.

Turning up the volume, I listen to her melodious voice as it pours through the speakers, throaty and husky and sexy as sin. My eyes drink her in, clad in a long, flowy dress, her eyes bright and gleaming, filled with so much soul and emotion. Her hair wraps around her shoulders in beach waves, the feather tattoo on her hand winking as she grips the microphone. Her entire being embraces the music.

But after the first few lines, I lean closer to my screen, studying Everly. An undercurrent in her voice pulls at me, tugs at something I can't put my finger on. On screen, a guitar is smashed, a tumbler of whisky flung against the wall, the glass shattering, the shards falling to the floor in slow motion. Lee's eyes bleed pain, her petite frame melting with anguish.

THE FIRST TIME I saw you,
My heart soared the skies above.
The first time you kissed me,
My mind was thinking love.
And we danced and laughed,
Dared destiny and courted fate.
We dreamed and we loved
Until love turned to hate.
Because you broke me down
with words that cut too deep to heal.
You crushed my spirit
Until I couldn't even feel.
The bite of your teeth against my neck,
Your fingers digging into my skin.
The bruise of your unyielding kiss,

the scent of your cologne pure gin.
And we danced and laughed,
Dared destiny and courted fate.
We dreamed and we loved
Until love turned to hate.
You've stripped away my confidence,
Stomped on my pride.
Stolen all of my self-worth,
And now I can't confide
In the friends who still reach out
And call from time to time.
What you've done to me
surely is a crime.
And we danced and laughed,
Dared destiny and courted fate.
We dreamed and we loved
Until love turned to hate.
I used to believe in fairytales
Until you rewrote our ending.
Now, I don't believe in anything,
And baby it's a blessing.
And we danced and laughed,
Dared destiny and courted fate.
We dreamed and we loved
Until love turned to hate.
Until love turned to hate.

The song ends and I sit still, confusion rocking through me. But the greatest emotion, the one that eats all the others for breakfast, is fear.

What the fuck? Who is she talking about? An ex? Corey Hughes? No one? Just a fictional character written by someone else to make a hit song?

Recalling the concerned doctor in the emergency room, the way he slipped Everly his card, I listen to the song two more times. Even though I can't prove anything, something serious nags at me.

Did someone hurt Everly? Is that the real reason she's here in Edinburgh, alone?

Ignoring the fact that the coffee is cold, I take a large gulp, just for something to do with my hands.

No, that doesn't make any sense. She would tell someone, confide in her friends. Right?

Oh God, what if this is her telling someone? Telling the whole fucking world and no one understands, no one reaches out.

Simmer down, mate. You're making a hell of a lot of assumptions.

But what about the scars on her hip? The way she backed away when she thought I was angry?

My body tightens until my limbs literally ache from the tension. The thought of someone putting his hands on her, hurting her, it rips me up from the inside out. A violent shudder runs through me and I see red, my mind concocting the worst scenarios. The type that nightmares are made of.

What did she say to me her first day here?

She's "hiding out."

What if she really is?

What if she's crying out for help, and no one, not even me, is listening?

"Hey superstar," I greet Everly as she slides into the passenger seat of my car.

Leaning over the center console, she kisses my cheek. "Hey yourself." She holds up a pastry bag. "I brought dessert."

"You didn't have to bring anything." I reach over, placing a hand on her thigh. Underneath my touch, she stiffens, a ripple of something flashing across her face. But in the next breath, she relaxes, her expression composed once more.

Am I just imagining things now? Or did she really panic for a second when I touched her? Am I searching for signs?

Just ask her about the song.

Pulling onto the main street, I grip the steering wheel. "I need to warn you, or prepare you is probably a better word, but Daisy, Finn's girlfriend, referred to herself as one of your fan-girls."

Everly laughs. "I'm flattered."

"Aye, well, I'm not sure the rest of my family even knows who you are other than a girl I dated in uni, so don't get a big head about it."

"I wouldn't dream of it."

"Daisy's favorite song is 'Mending Broken.'" I toss out as a feeler, glancing at Everly.

She turns to look out the window, and my fingers tighten around the steering wheel.

"It was a lucrative single." Her voice is steady, her tone disinterested.

"Did you write it?"

"Bits and pieces. It was more of a collaboration."

"Oh."

"Yeah. Hey, where's Livvy?" She turns to look in the backseat. "I got some new polish colors for her to try out."

"Aunt Jenni picked her up from school today, so Liv could help her with dinner. I think Aunt Jenni just really misses her since Liv was in Paris all of July, and Aunt Jenni was in New York for August visiting Sierra and the baby."

Everly relaxes into the passenger seat, turning her attention to me once more. "That's nice that they're so close."

"It's a blessing, that's what it is. Olivia could really use a strong female presence; someone she could look up to as a role model."

"I'm glad she has your Aunt Jenni." *Is her tone sharper than usual?*

"Me too."

"Are any of your cousins going to be at dinner? I feel like I know them, even though we've never met.

Your stories from way back when were quite vivid with all of your pranks and goofing off."

I grin, thinking about Lachlan, Callum, and Liam. "Honestly, I'm not sure. Liam is at boarding school in Glasgow. Since the term just started, he probably won't be around, but he sometimes surprises his mum. And Lachlan and Callum both work out of the London office. If they were in Edinburgh, they would have come by work today, but you never know."

"Got it."

"But I promise you Daisy will make enough of a splash that it will feel like more people."

"I can't wait to meet her."

"Famous last words."

"I CAN'T BELIEVE it's really you!" Daisy pulls the door to Aunt Jenni's house wide open, as if she was standing at the entrance and peering out the window, awaiting our arrival.

"I'm happy to meet you, Daisy." Everly steps forward and envelops Daisy in a hug.

Over Everly's shoulder, Daisy widens her eyes at me, her body going completely still. For a moment, I think she's going to cry.

"Breathe, Dais," Finn says from the entrance to the kitchen.

"I'm trying." Daisy sniffles and Everly chuckles.

"Hey there, little love." I catch Olivia as she zooms around the corner and jumps into my arms.

"Daddy, I'm so happy you brought Everly," she whispers in my ear.

"Do you think Daisy can handle it?" I ask her.

She turns and looks at Daisy's face, bright red with embarrassment, wearing a goofy-ass grin, her eyes wide and unblinking.

"Nope."

"Me either." I kiss my daughter's forehead before putting her down.

She walks over to Everly and offers her a simple hug. "I need to show you my new ballet routine."

"I can't wait to see it." Everly bends down to Olivia's height and pulls some nail varnish from her purse. "New colors for our pedicures."

"Ooh, they're so pretty and sparkly!" Olivia beams, taking the bottles from Everly's hand. "Thanks, Everly."

"See? How normal people act?" I tell Daisy, gesturing toward Olivia and Everly.

"You don't get me at all," Daisy responds as Finn chuckles.

"Aaron, is that you?" Aunt Jenni calls out, walking into the foyer, wiping her hands on her apron. "Hi dear," she greets me, kissing my cheek. Turning toward Everly, she smiles warmly. "And you must be Everly." She takes Everly's hands in her own. "It's so good to meet you." She steers Everly out of the foyer and into the kitchen. "Can I get you something to drink? Water? Tea? Something stronger to deal with those crazies?"

Everly's laughter, warm and sincere, floats behind her, spilling into the foyer.

At the sound, some of my doubts and assumptions subside.

Just enjoy dinner.

12

🎵 everly 🎤

Aaron's family is pure warmth.

Like the caring, thoughtful, generous kind who make room for you at their table and insist that you always have a place there. Aunt Jenni and Uncle James —I've mentally adopted them as my own—are lively, welcoming, and straight up my aspirational couple for my retirement years. Not that Uncle James is retired but… still.

"Oh, thank you so much for bringing dessert." Aunt Jenni places the pie I brought down in the center of the table.

"You're taking over Daisy's job," Uncle James jokes, patting the top of Daisy's head. "Don't forget to bring those cupcakes I like to the office on Monday."

"Done," Daisy agrees. "Everly, you have to try these cupcakes. They are amazing."

"Here we go," Finn groans. "Dais, you can't pretend the places that have American owners have better baked goods."

"Of course she can." Aunt Jenni grins.

Daisy rolls her eyes. "I'm not, Finn. I really think Everly will love the cupcakes."

"What place is it?" I ask, taking a sip of the coffee Aunt Jenni prepared.

As Daisy launches into a story about the bakery she frequents and their incredible cupcakes, Aaron catches my eye. His smile is subtle, but his eyes speak a million truths. They're bright, happy, and filled with a hopeful contentment I haven't experienced since we were in college.

Having him look at me so purely is a punch in the gut, a quick reminder of what was, what we once shared and squandered. People always say it won't last when high school sweethearts marry or college students fall in love, and maybe it wouldn't have with Aaron and me.

Maybe that's why the universe kept us apart for so many years. So that we would have the time to explore and dream and achieve our goals. But tonight, sitting with his family, around a large harvest table with him next to me, his hand drifting to my thigh, I feel hopeful, too. Maybe this is our second chance, a fresh start, the do-over I desperately want.

"I'll definitely try them." I grin at Daisy, the cupcake aficionado.

"Hey, anyone home?" a voice calls from the doorway.

"Oh!" Aunt Jenni jumps up, clasping her hands together.

"It's Lach," Livvy yells, running from the kitchen to greet Aaron's cousin. "I missed you, Lachy!"

"There she is," Lachlan exclaims, walking into the kitchen a few moments later, Olivia hanging off his hip like a Koala bear. "What's going on here?" He grins, bending to kiss his mom's cheek and stooping to wrap an arm around Uncle James's shoulders in a half-hug.

"Family dinner," Livvy says, clasping his face in between her palms and forcing him to look at her. "Dad invited Everly. We're supposed to be on our best behavior, so we don't scare her away."

Lachlan throws his head back and laughs. "Did Daddy tell you that, princess?"

Livvy shakes her head. "No. Daisy."

Across from me, Daisy blushes and ducks her head, avoiding Finn's gaze.

Standing from the table, I extend a hand. "Hi. I'm Everly."

Lachlan ignores my hand and scoops me into a hug with his free arm. "I know who you are. It's good to finally meet you."

"Listening to that country twang on the side, Lach?" Finn teases.

Lachlan grins, depositing Olivia on her seat, and gripping the back of her chair. "Hardly." His eyes cut to me, open and friendly. "No offense."

"No worries, it's not for everyone," I agree.

"I'm here on a secret mission," Lachlan admits, slipping into an empty chair. "Thanks." He accepts a glass of wine from his step-dad.

"What's that?" Aaron asks curiously. "Something happening in the London office?"

Across from me, Daisy busies herself with eating her second slice of pie, her eyes trained on the plate.

"Uh-oh," Finn mutters. "Daisy Kane?"

Daisy shovels a forkful of pie into her mouth.

Lachlan, Olivia, Aunt Jenni, and Uncle James laugh.

Next to me, Aaron squeezes my knee. Nerves begin to skate up my spine. What's going on? Is this some type of prank that I'm missing? My skin flushes, and I feel heat crawl up my neck.

"What's the mission?" I ask Lachlan.

"You," he says simply. "And Aaron." He reaches over and takes a bite of my pie like it's the most natural thing in the world, like we're old friends. Returning my fork to my plate, he picks up my napkin and wipes his mouth. I decide I like him and his unapologetic boldness. "Excellent choice on the pie. Sierra will be pleased that it's apple."

Aaron groans next to me.

"Someone fill me in?" I ask, my eyes darting to Daisy.

She blushes tomato red and mouths, "Sorry."

Lachlan wraps a hand around the back of my chair, leaning closer and dropping his voice. "That girl," he says, pointing to Daisy, "is my sister's best friend."

"Sierra," I confirm.

"Yes, the two of them should be in their eighties, at a senior club, playing bingo and bitching about their health issues, with the way they gossip."

I crack a grin, finally understanding where this conversation is headed. "So you've been sent to scope me out."

"Exactly."

"You know, I could be the enemy, right? Why are you so open regarding your mission?"

"Because," Lachlan's tone is serious, his expression giving nothing away, "you brought pie. Everyone knows pie is my favorite." At this, he grins, and the rest of his family laughs.

"Lachlan," Daisy whines, throwing a napkin at him. "Way to throw me under the bus."

Lach shrugs. "That's what you get for riling my sister up with all this chatter about Aaron dating a famous singer and his 'rekindling' a relationship." Lachlan tosses air-quotes around "rekindling," and Daisy drops her forehead to the table in embarrassment.

Next to her, Finn shakes with laughter. "You got caught, love. Best to own it."

"Sorry, Everly." Daisy's voice is muffled.

"I'm flattered, really." I let her off the hook, grinning at Aaron. Because the truth is, I am. Aaron's family welcomes me not because of my career or wealth, but because they want Aaron to be happy. And if that isn't the definition of family, I don't know what is. "You know, you should report back with something scandalous," I mock whisper to Lachlan, whose eyebrows rise with amusement.

"I'm listening." He dips his chin toward me, swiping my entire plate of pie and digging in.

Livvy giggles next to him, and he turns and taps her nose with his finger.

"Something good and juicy," I say.

"Tell Sierra that Everly is moving here permanently, and her and my brother are eloping," Finn suggests as Daisy's eyes nearly fall out of her head.

Aunt Jenni gasps and a long moment of awkward silence hovers over the table. Aaron jerks next to me before his body goes still.

Oh shit, I shouldn't have said anything at all.

Luckily, Daisy knows how to handle these situations, even if she has to throw herself under the bus. "Can you imagine?" She leans forward over the table, tucking her honey-brown hair behind her ears. "Then, we would be sisters!"

Crickets.

"Oh please, Finn. One day, you will propose. How could you not want to marry me?" she adds, and the laughter starts up all over again.

"Are you sure Olivia wants to sleep at Finn and Daisy's place tonight?" I ask Aaron hours later, settling back against the couch cushions in his living room.

After dessert at Aunt Jenni's, the guys all retired to the den to watch rugby while I helped Daisy and Aunt Jenni clear away the plates. We chatted easily, with Aunt Jenni and Daisy leading the conversation and gushing over Sierra's new baby girl, Luna Mae. Everything about the experience was comforting and natural and more than I anticipated.

The only downside is knowing I won't have many more family dinners like that. I need to return to Nashville soon, and the more I entwine my life with Aaron's, the harder it's going to be. My chest aches at the thought of having to say goodbye at all.

"Are you kidding me? She jumps at any chance to sleep at their flat. Finn will build a huge fort with her, and Daisy will polish her nails and toes with the new varnish you bought her. And sparkles."

"Sparkles are the holy grail when you're seven."

"Tell me about it. Here you go." Aaron hands me a tumbler with three fingers of whisky.

"Cheers." I hold my glass up to his, as he leans forward in the chair next to the couch.

"To all your success and all your future dreams." His eyes hold mine as he sips his whisky, and I flush at his words, my skin heating under the intensity of his stare.

"Thank you for tonight. Your family is really special. I had a good time."

"Me too. It was better than I thought," he admits.

"Right?" I agree. "I was so nervous but everything seemed so…"

"Natural."

"Organic."

We grin at each other, and a zing zips through my body at the spark in his gaze, a slow burn of heat I want to melt into, a flicker of longing that feeds all the malnourished parts of my soul.

"I could lose myself here," I admit, smacking my lips together, the whiskey smooth as it rolls over my tongue.

"Lose yourself?"

"You know what I mean. Reinvent myself. Start over."

"Are things really that hectic for you in Tennessee? I mean, I know your career must be go-go-go all the time, but it's what you want, isn't it?" He leans forward again, resting his elbows on his knees, his eyes boring into mine like he needs to know that yes, my career has been fulfilling.

"Most days, yes."

"And the other days?"

"The other days, I wish I chose a different path."

"Like what?" he asks, but his tone holds an edge, like he already knows he's not going to like my answer.

"Why'd you really do it? End things between us?"

Aaron's expression darkens, his jaw clenching. Regret flickers in the centers of his eyes, an icy blue, the part of the flame that lures you closer, but burns you the worst. "I wanted you to pursue the career you've always dreamed of."

"And you didn't think that was possible if I was dating you? You know, loads of people in the music industry manage to have relationships."

"I know. But we were young, you were starting out, and I was always going to come home and work at Anderson. What did you want me to do? Ask you to forget your dream and move to Edinburgh? Country music doesn't really have a scene here." He throws his arm wide to encompass his apartment, his city, the entire country of Scotland.

"I know," I admit. "It's a relief, I guess."

"What is?"

"Knowing you broke my heart for me and not because of me."

His brow furrows, anger blazing across his features and turning his jaw to a razor's edge and his eyes glacial. "You thought I didn't want to be with you?" His words are whispered, but they're anything but soft.

"I was nineteen, and the boy I loved shattered me."

His arm reaches over the couch's armrest, so his fingers can encircle my wrist. "I was so fucking in love with you, Lee, I couldn't see straight. But I didn't want you to ever resent me, resent us. Maybe you did anyway. But forgetting your dreams, ignoring your calling, throwing all of your hard work away to follow a boy at nineteen was never supposed to be your story."

"How do you know my story turned out the way it was supposed to?"

"You were nominated for a Grammy."

"I didn't win."

"You will next time," he says the words with so much certainty that I can't stop the small smile from spreading across my lips.

"You've always believed in my dreams, sometimes even more than me. I love music; it's in my blood, and songwriting is my greatest passion. But sometimes, when your passion becomes your work and is funneled into a business that you can't control, it's exhausting."

"Do you have to go back?"

"Yeah. My tour kicks off in January. The fact that I'm still here is... concerning. My manager is desperate for me to return to Nashville, mainly to get my ass in gear for the tour, but also because she's my best friend."

"Addison?"

"Yeah. Addi is pretty amazing. We've been a team for a long time."

"How long is your tour?"

"Three months. Across the entire US with some stops in Canada."

"Are you allowed visitors on this tour?" He stands from his perch on the chair before shifting into the space next to me. His fingers reach out, tracing the feather tattooed on my hand.

"Don't even get my hopes up."

"Because Olivia and I have some free time in February."

I grin at him, my heart cracking wide open at the realization that he is invested in us, wants to explore our possibilities for real. "I would love nothing more than for you guys to crash my tour. If you come, I'll even bring y'all up on stage."

Aaron chuckles, his fingers leaving my hand to toy with my hair. I shift my weight, tucking my legs underneath me, and turn my face toward his. "I'm serious."

"So am I." His breath caresses the shell of my ear, causing a shiver to shimmy down my back.

Biting my lower lip, I study his gaze. "We're really doing this?" My voice is breathier than I intend, as the heat in Aaron's eyes expands, his face drawing closer.

"We've been doing this since I first saw you at The Fringe."

"Aaron, I sprained my ankle at The Fringe." My fingers hook under his collar, my thumb tracing the top button of his shirt, skirting upward to press against his Adam's apple.

"And we got the chance to get reacquainted," he continues, dropping his hands to my hips and tugging so I slide down the couch, my body spread out under his.

"At the hospital." I snort, glancing down at our physical position, Aaron's knee settling between my thighs.

He chuckles, the sound warm and rich, but his eyes blaze as they drink me in. "It doesn't matter how it started; it matters that it's real. And this is just the tip of the iceberg, Lee. I knew the moment I tasted you." He dips his head, brushing his lips against mine so faintly, I arch upward to chase his kiss. "I'd want it all," he admits on a breath that hovers for a millisecond between us until his mouth crashes back down over mine, putting me out of my misery, and dousing me in desire so strong, I'm not sure it could ever burn out.

Gripping his biceps, I squeeze until he shifts back. My hands slide up to his shoulders, entwine behind his neck. I pull myself up until he's forced to shift his weight, so I can slide into his lap. Aaron tugs me into his frame, never breaking our connection, until I'm straddling him, my inner thighs gripping his hips, his fingers scraping against the back of my head.

Our mouths clash, at war with each other, our tongues waging a massive assault.

"Goddamn I've missed you." He breathes.

"It's only been two days."

"Two days too long."

Sighing into his mouth, Aaron nips at my lower lip. His hands squeeze my waist, his fingertips digging into my hips as I grind against him. My hands tug his hair, my elbows hooking over his shoulders. I bite down on his tongue and he yelps, pulling back slightly, a gleam in his eyes.

Moving us to the floor, he lays me down, right in the center of his living room, sheltered between the coffee table and the couch. Pressing kisses down the column of my neck, my body craves his touch, my soul his caress.

The first time, on his dining table, our connection was like a homecoming, sweet and soulful and pure. Since then, it's been everything in between. But right now, this, this is anything but sweet. It's passionate and desire-filled, with his hands claiming me as his and my mouth branding him as mine.

His moves are surer, his hands steadier, but the way he lights me up, makes me burn and yearn and crave, is the same wildness I've only ever felt with him.

Goosebumps skate over my skin, followed by blazing heat. Arching into his touch, I rain open-mouthed kisses over his jawline, down his neck, across the top of his chest. His groans fill the air, spurring me on and healing other wounds, other hurts, in the same breath.

Unbuttoning his shirt, I grin at him. "You never used to dress this fancy."

"You always used to look this beautiful."

Leaning forward, I capture his lips with mine, slowing down the pace. Sliding his shirt off his shoulders, it pools to the floor behind him. My palms glide over his chest, sinking lower to his abdomen, desperate to touch every inch of him, desperate to get lost in a dream I've never forgotten.

Aaron's hands dip into my waist and skim up my ribcage. He pushes my cardigan off my shoulders and hooks his fingers around the delicate straps of my dress, slipping it off until it drops to my waist. I sit before him, topless, save for the strands of turquoise beads that drape around my neck.

Aaron groans, dropping his forehead to my shoulder. Looking back up, his eyes gleam with an unmatched boldness, a reckless need. "Lee, I need you to know that I'm not giving up this time. I'm not backing away. I'm not letting you go so easily."

"So keep me." The words fall from my lips. "That past is in the past for us, Aar. Start writing our future," I whisper into his mouth.

And he does.

IT'S LATE, or early depending on your sense of time, when I slide out from under Aaron's duvet cover and head to the kitchen for a glass of water. The cool air sends a chill through my body as I leave the warmth of Aaron's bed, his naked body sprawled in the center. Sleeping on his stomach, an arm curled underneath his pillow, his face looks boyish. A pang hits the center of my chest as he looks so much like he used to, just a kid with a too-big heart and pride in his responsibilities.

Padding to the kitchen, I fill a glass with water and grab my phone off the counter.

Glancing down at the message that lights up the screen, my breath freezes in my throat. Dread fills my veins, fear clogs my vision, and adrenaline spikes in my blood stream as I whip my head around, as if *he's* here. As if *he* knows where I am and has found me and is right here, right now, in Aaron's apartment.

> Corey: Baby, please come home. We can fix this, put it behind us. I miss you, Everly. I need you.

Panic wells in my chest at Corey's message. Followed by guilt. And shame. Jesus, why can't I break his hold on me? Cowering, I slide to the floor, the glass of water and my phone clenched in my fists. Even nearly four thousand miles away, Corey can inspire the fight or flight mode.

Fuck. Dropping my head back, I consider flight. Consider leaving right now, without even writing a note, and disappearing.

Aaron's snore fills the quiet of his apartment.

Tears sting the back of my throat, causing pain with each swallow.

Fuck this. I'm done hiding. I'm done running.

It's time I start living my best life for myself.

Deleting the message, I send a silent fuck you to Corey Hughes.

And ignore him and his message completely.

13

aaron

The left side of my bed is empty when I wake in the morning, the sweet scent of Everly's perfume still clinging to the pillowcases.

"Lee?" I call out, swinging my legs to the edge of my bed and pulling on a pair of joggers.

No response.

Standing up, I walk into the kitchen, check the living room, even pass by the bathroom. But the entire flat is eerily quiet. Everly's purse is gone.

As is she.

What the hell? My stomach dips as an irrational wave of fear rushes through my body.

Did something happen?

Is she okay?

Is she hurt?

Thoughts ricochet in my mind and even though a logical part of me knows I'm overreacting, fear wavers on the periphery of my mind.

The ringing of my cell phone jars me out of my head, and I pick up immediately.

"Hey man, how was your night?" Finn asks.

"My night was pretty awesome. Except I just woke up and Everly is gone."

"Gone? What do you mean?"

"She's not here."

Finn is quiet for several moments before he bursts out laughing. "No way! She ghosted you? I knew I liked her."

"Fuck off. I'm worried—"

The door to my flat swings open, and Everly steps inside, balancing a tray with two coffees and holding a bakery bag. "Mornin' sleepyhead. I borrowed your keys," she explains, dropping them into a small dish I keep by the front door.

"She's here with breakfast," I tell my brother, relief filling my chest like a balloon. I blow out an exhale, pinching the bridge of my nose. *Why the hell did I panic?* "How's Livvy?"

"She's great. Daisy took her to the park."

"I'll swing by to pick her up in a little bit." My eyes are glued to Everly, watching as she moves around my kitchen, pulling out plates and utensils, folding napkins. She knows the space as well as I do, and I like it, like seeing her in my flat like she belongs here. Deep down, I know she does. *Does she realize it, too?*

"Take your time."

Ending the call, I toss my phone onto the kitchen island and step behind Everly, wrapping my arms around her hips and pulling her flush against my chest.

At first, she stiffens, her body locking down, and I start to pull back, concerned at her reaction. But after a moment, she relaxes, shimmying her ass against me until I groan. "How hungry are you?"

She snorts, twirling in my arms until she's facing me, her back pressed against the kitchen countertop, my arms caging her in. "Depends what you're proposing?" She grins playfully, but a shadow moves through her eyes.

Dropping my forehead to hers, I breathe her in, note the quickening of her pulse in her throat. "What's wrong, Lee?"

She pauses, lifting her head, so I'm forced to look into her eyes. "What do you mean?"

"You seem nervous."

"Do I?"

I nod, frowning at her weak attempt at deflection.

"I am."

"Why?" I whisper, relieved that she's being honest with me, worried that I'm going to hate what she says next. Especially after such an incredible night, one where I felt like we were turning a corner.

"Because I don't want this to end." Her hands slide up my arms until they're settled on my shoulders. "Now, tell me again what you were going to propose we do instead of eating breakfast?"

Grinning down at her, I hoist her up, my hands palming her ass as she hooks her legs around my waist. "What do you think?" I ask, walking her to my bedroom. Tossing her in the center of my bed, she giggles, and I catch a glimpse of the carefree girl she was years ago.

Wrapping my hands around her ankles, I pull until she's spread out beneath me. Crawling up her frame, I drop kisses to every inch of exposed skin. "I thought you ducked out when I woke up and you were gone," I admit, hating the neediness in my tone.

Everly reaches down, her hands bracketing my face until I'm forced to look at her. She shakes her head. "I'm here, Aaron. For as long as I can stay, I will."

I know she says the words to provide comfort, but all they do is remind me that the clock is running out, and soon I'll have to make a move one way or the other.

That we need to have some difficult conversations and settle on a compromise that works for both of us.

Because she can't stay right now, and I can't be away from her forever.

THE FOLLOWING WEEK, our lives meld together all over again. Old habits and patterns settle into place, and I find myself craving her more than I ever have before. Not just her body, but her presence, her energy, her place by my side. Each day, she spends more time at my flat, eating dinner with Olivia and me, helping Liv with a homework assignment, putting away the cups and dishes, as I tuck my daughter into bed.

Yet something nags at me. Most of the time when I glance at Everly, she smiles back, her expression serene, her mouth soft enough to kiss. But other times, the moments where she doesn't catch my eye, I note the way her fingers twist together, how she bites the corner of her mouth, her eyes guarded, and her expression uncertain.

And I can't help but wonder if she's unsure of me, of us, or just worried for our impending separation while she's on tour? Whatever it is, it has a stream of unease flowing through me, making me desperate to settle our future plans and status.

"Damn, you've become so serious," Lachlan announces the following Monday, entering my office and sliding into the vacant chair.

"You're back so soon?" I raise my eyebrows. Normally, Lachlan, or my other cousin Callum, will pop into the Edinburgh office whenever a work-related issue demands their attention. But they're rarely in town for more than a few days.

"Yeah." Lach grips the back of his neck, averting his gaze.

"Is everything okay?"

"Think so," he mutters. "Anyway, how are things with you and CMT's sweetheart?"

"What the hell is CMT?"

Lachlan rolls his eyes. "Country Music Television. You know, for someone so in love with this girl, you don't seem to know much about her life."

"Who says I'm in love with her?" I challenge, raising my eyebrows.

"Please." My cousin laughs, slapping the edge of my desk. "It's stamped all over both of your faces. Let me guess, you haven't said it yet?"

I shake my head, not wanting to have this conversation with Lachlan but not wanting to seek out Finn, either. In times like these, I'm grateful for Daisy, even though she tends to meddle.

"You should," Lach continues, and something about the serious note in the tone of his voice when it's almost always just joking and ribbing from him, gives me pause.

"Why's that?"

"You don't let the real deal slip away. And you already did once." My cousin clears his throat. "You're a lucky son of a bitch to have a second shot. Don't take that lightly."

"I'm not." I sound defensive.

"Good." Lachlan's gaze bores into mine, his dark eyes from his Native-American heritage on his father's side turn pitch black with a graveness he's never shown before.

"What's going on with you?"

He sighs, blowing out a long exhale. "A lot of crap I don't want to get into now. Just square things away with

Everly. Don't leave them up to chance again."

"Okay."

Lachlan stands. "I wanted to say goodbye. I'm flying out in a few hours. Just stopped by to have lunch with James."

"All right. Well, I'll see you soon, then."

"Yeah. I'll be back for American Thanksgiving."

"Oh, I love your mum's Thanksgiving dinner."

"Tell me about it." Lachlan grins, looking more like himself. "Take care, Aar."

"You too," I tell my cousin, still thrown by his strange demeanor.

Waiting until he closes my office door, I can't help but think about his words. Everly and I do need to make some decisions. We've been putting off asking the difficult questions, offering the honest answers, but each day that passes brings her closer to her flight back to Nashville. And Lachlan's right. I can't let her leave again without making sure she's knows I want her to come home to me when her tour is finished.

She's it for me. I've made a lot of mistakes in the past where Everly was concerned and afterwards with Kate. Now, I'm bloody paying for them, but I've learned my lessons the hard way. I won't make the same mistakes by keeping quiet, by leaving things up to chance. Everly needs to know exactly how I feel about her, what type of future I want with her, and that she's the one calling the shots this time around.

Even if it breaks my heart.

Even if it kills me.

She'll have to be the one to end things between us.

Because I'm not letting her go again.

14
♫ everly 🎤

Pacing back and forth in front of my bed, I clench my phone in my fist. Why is he messaging me now? Why does he keep popping up at the worst possible times? For over two months, radio silence. And now, two messages in one week. Does he really know where I am? Has he found me?

Fear skates down my spine as I delete his message.

What is he planning if he knows where I am and hasn't come for me yet? Corey is a sneaky son of a bitch, and prone to theatrics the way he is, he's playing at something with his stupid messages.

I just don't know what his angle is.

And the not knowing causes dread to settle over me, shadow all my interactions, and filter into all of my thoughts.

The shrill ringing of my phone has me jumping, cold

beads of sweat dotting my hairline, but I sigh in relief when Addison's face appears on the screen.

"Hey Addi."

"Top of the mornin' to ye."

"That's Irish, I think. And it's already afternoon here."

"Close enough. How are you and the sexy sin you're knockin' boots with?"

"You definitely peaked in the nineties."

Addi chuckles. "What's happening with Aaron?"

"Things are good. Great really. He's planning to visit me on tour."

"Oh wow," Addison says, her voice cautious like usual. "How do you feel about that?"

"Is that even a serious question?"

"Just be careful, Everly. A lot of things can change in a short amount of time."

"I know. You're right. But please, stop with the gloom and doom. Just be my best friend and be happy for me."

"You're right. I am happy for you, honestly. I just, I can't help but worry after everything…"

"I know," I whisper.

"But enough gloom and doom, I'm calling with the best news ever." Excitement laces her tone.

"What's going on?"

"Oh, you know, just some upcoming opportunities you may be interested in."

"Such as?" I sit on the edge of my bed, nerves ping-ponging around my chest.

"A performance at the Grand Ole Opry."

"Shut up!" I exclaim, jumping back up. Feeling the grin that splits my face, I laugh as Addi repeats herself. "When? How?"

"Apparently, you're in high demand. And even taking some time off hasn't diminished that. November 30. Don't pass this up, Ev. This is a once in a lifetime."

I nod, squealing. "Dance party?" I switch our call to FaceTime.

"Duh!"

On screen, Addi and I break out in an impromptu dance party, shaking our asses and celebrating this huge milestone. She's positively giddy with excitement, infusing me with renewed appreciation for my career choice, for my life, for every sacrifice I had to make to get to this point. The Grand Ole Opry!

"I'll be there."

"Good. You shouldn't let him take anything else away from you." She collapses in her desk chair. "You haven't heard from him, have you?"

Damn. How the hell did she know that? "Just a few text messages. How'd you know?" I narrow my gaze, shuddering.

"I saw him the other day at Teddi's," she confesses, referencing a restaurant we used to frequent. "He was with Annabeth," Addison spits out, foaming with her hatred for Corey. Annabeth is another woman in the industry; someone he works with in a professional capacity… and fucks on the side. You'd think I'd be jealous or hate that my boyfriend has a side piece but truthfully, when I first learned about Annabeth, all I felt was relief. How messed up is that? Still, Corey is smart. He can't be seen out around town with any random woman, but Annabeth doesn't raise eyebrows since her and Corey collaborate on various projects. "But he seemed, I don't know, smug. Like he knows something, has information about you, something. He's up to something, Everly."

"He always is." I breathe out, my stomach sinking with the confirmation for what I've known all along: I'll never truly be free of Corey Hughes. Glancing at myself in the mirror on the back of my closet door, I study my appearance. Green eyes that sparkle, long, brown, wavy hair, a slender frame. To a passing person, I'd look like a regular, normal, relatively happy thirty-three-year-old. But under my tanned skin and bright smile lie the scars that no one sees, that no one even guesses at. And Corey is the master at picking those wounds back open.

"Everly, what he did to you is inexcusable. It's not too late to—"

"No. It's fine. Let's leave it alone, Addi. Please. I can't lose everything I've worked for. I'm not going to sabotage my career. "

She sighs, and silence hangs between us.

"How is he?" I ask, hating that I'm still curious, that he crosses my mind at all.

Addison rolls her eyes, removing the cat's-eyes glasses she wears to pinch the bridge of her nose. "He's the same as always. A bullshitting con artist."

"What is he saying about me?"

"Everly Pierce, you can't seriously care about—"

"I don't. I mean, what is he telling people?"

"He's not stepping out with anyone publicly. Instead, he's still playing the role of victim, telling anyone who will listen that you just up and left him with no reason, and he is devastated. Heartbroken."

"Bastard," I whisper through clenched teeth, seething inside.

"Come home, Everly. Not for him. Not for anyone but yourself."

"November 30. The Opry," I confirm.

"Good." Addi grins, the right side of her mouth ticking up a millimeter higher than the left. "Let me know once you book your flight and anything you need."

"I will. Thanks for the amazing news, Addi."

"You deserve it all, babe."

I end the call and toss my phone onto my bed. The Grand Ole Opry! I pinch myself, closing my eyes and breathing in the satisfaction I feel in this moment. The Grand Ole Opry…

He's been drinking.

I know it the moment the door closes, and I hear his footfalls in the hallway. They sound different when he's drunk. Heavier. Angrier.

It's not uncommon for Corey to have a drink or two after a long day, but lately it's more like five or six drinks. Every day.

"There's my sunshine," he slurs when he enters the kitchen, wrapping an arm around my waist and pressing a kiss to my temple.

"Hi babe. How was your day?" I ask, picking up tongs to toss the salad.

"Why don't you tell me, Ev?" He leans back against the countertop, his ankles crossed. But his stance is too defensive, his smile leering. Something is off.

"I'm not sure what you mean," I begin cautiously, keeping my eyes trained on the romaine lettuce.

Corey laughs, the sound bitter. Hard. "You don't?"

I shake my head.

"You don't know that Mitch called me this afternoon and told me that you and his wife, Laurie, went out for drinks last week?"

"Laurie and I are friends. She invited me to meet her. What's the big deal?"

"The big deal? God, Everly, are you really so naive? Everyone in this town knows Laurie cheats on Mitch. Do you want everyone to think you're a slut, too?"

I flinch at Corey's harshness.

"Or worse, that I'm not just fucking a slut but also shacking up with her? You're so goddamn selfish sometimes, you know that? Did you even think about my reputation?" He steps closer, the scent of gin strong on his breath. His hand fists my hair and he *pulls, yanking my head back so my neck is completely exposed.*

Shivering, I hate that I'm in such a vulnerable position. I hate that he's made me as vulnerable as I am.

"Did you?" he jeers.

I shake my head, unable to form words.

"I can ruin you, Everly. I can make it so no one in Nashville knows your fucking name. You were nothing before you met me, and you'll return to nothing if you ever think of jeopardizing my reputation again. Do you understand me?"

"Yes," I whisper.

"Can't hear you, babe." He pulls my hair harder and I yelp, feeling him growing hard behind me.

"Yes."

"Good." He releases me. "Now, what are we having for dinner?"

Digging the heels of my palms into my eyes, I try to erase the images in my mind, block out the voice that disrupts my waking and sleeping hours, even now.

Corey Hughes, country music executive and big shot, my ex-boyfriend, the man who beat me so badly I ran away to Edinburgh.

He used to hang my career over my head all the time.

But now look, I scored an opportunity to perform at the Grand Ole Opry without him. I did it on my own, with my reputation, my talent. I don't need him. I never did.

Except…

The timing of everything causes my steps to falter, forces me to sink to the edge of my bed and think things through. *Be logical, Everly. Remove all emotion and focus on the facts.*

Emotions trip people up, cause people to make stupid mistakes. And in my position, I can't afford any mistakes. Ever.

Corey's sent me two messages in the past week, one of those messages today. Just a day after Addison and him ran into each other at Teddi's. The same day Addison called me with news about the Grand Ole Opry.

Is it really a coincidence?

Or did Corey have a hand in creating this opportunity?

Is he trying to lure me home?

Does he even have that type of power, of sway, with the Grand Ole Opry?

Does it even matter?

How could I consider passing up this opportunity?

Sure, going means I'll have to see Corey again.

But not going means losing more pieces of myself.

And I'm not willing to compromise myself anymore.

My time in Edinburgh, with Aaron, has reminded me of who I once was, has convinced me again that I'm still worth it.

And this time, I'm not giving up on myself.

Walking out of my room, I jump at a knock on the door.

Pressing the heel of my palm into the center of my chest, I close my eyes and count to ten, inhaling and exhaling slowly. My nerves are scattered around my feet and suddenly, I'm petrified of what, or who, waits for me on the other side of the door.

Is he here?

Has he come for me?

The knock sounds again, louder this time, and I shudder.

"Everly? You in there?"

"Dan?" I yelp, my relief overwhelming. Tears prick the corners of my eyes as I gulp the air, trying to get a grip.

You're fine. You're fine. You're fine.

"You okay?"

"Y-yes. One second." Pulling open the door, I grin at Dan. "What's going on?"

"Just wondering if you needed me tonight?"

"Oh, no, I'm all good, thanks. In fact, feel free to take a few days off, do some exploring, whatever you want."

"You sure? What about transportation?"

"I'm covered."

"With Aaron?"

I nod.

"You've been spending a lot of time with him, boss." Dan tilts his head, studying me.

"And?"

"I'm just saying, don't forget your life is in Nashville. Nashville will always pull you back." He says the words casually, but something about his word choice bothers me. Again. *Does he mean Nashville or Corey?*

Or am I overthinking everything now that Corey has popped back up?

Shaking my head, I offer Dan a smile. "I know. Just enjoying my time here while it lasts."

Dan shrugs. "Okay. Call me when you need me."

"Enjoy Edinburgh, Dan." I close the door, leaning against it and closing my eyes.

You're fine. You're fine. You're fine.

Because I like to torture myself, and because I'm looking for some type of reassurance that Corey isn't luring me back to Nashville on his terms, I fire up my laptop and check his social media accounts. Scrolling through his Facebook feed and clicking through his Instagram photos teaches me two things:

1. Corey Hughes is pretending that I'm still his girlfriend.

2. He'll never let me go.

15

aaron

"I have exciting news." Everly's eyes dazzle as she says the words, jade and sage and moss. But her posture, her fingers gripping the underside of the table-top, gives me pause. Her words and her gestures don't match, and the combination is jarring.

"What is it?" I ask, palming her hips to place a quick peck against her lips. I love coming home after a busy day at work to find her already here, sometimes cooking in the kitchen, other times playing with Olivia. Walking through the door to her has become one of my favorite parts of the day, and I hate knowing that my daily bright spot is going to dim soon with her departure.

"I've been invited to perform at the Grand Ole Opry!" She jumps up and down, her hands landing on my shoulders.

"That's fantastic, love," I gush back, grinning at her excitement, even though I have no idea what she's talking about.

"You don't know what that means, do you?"

I shake my head, biting back a chuckle. She's so adorable when she's excited like this. I love seeing her passion for her work play out across her features. "Tell me."

"It's, oh God, it's everything. Here." She pulls me over to the laptop sitting on my kitchen counter. Turning it on, she pulls up YouTube and begins to show me everything about her invitation.

"Damn Lee." I whistle low between my teeth. "I'm proud of you, love."

"Thanks!" She scrunches her nose, and I lean over to kiss it. "I'm really excited."

"This is incredible. You are so damn talented. I can't even wait to see you perform live. When is your performance?"

Her smile slips, as her eyes wander away from mine. "November 30."

I breathe in sharply. Two weeks. In two weeks, she'll be gone. "That's soon."

"Two weeks," she confirms.

"It's going to be incredible, though. You're going to be incredible." I rub the small of her back, dropping another kiss to the top of her head. Damn, I can't not touch her, not kiss her, when she's this close.

"You're not mad?" She glances back up, worrying her bottom lip between her teeth.

"Mad?" I chuckle. "Lee, I'm so in love with you, I could never be mad. Proud of your success? Always.

Sad you're going to have to leave? Of course. But mad? Never, love."

"What did you say?" she asks, her eyes widening, her words breathless.

"That I could never be angry with you," I say, teasing her.

"The first part."

"Oh that." I grin, cupping her cheek. "I love you, Everly Pierce. Have for a long fucking time. And I'm not going anywhere, even when you have to. So take your amazing opportunities and invitations and perform your heart out. But then I want you to come home to me."

"I love you," she says, dragging my face down to hers and kissing me with unexpected ferocity, like a claim. Her kiss pulls me under, soothes the disappointment I feel at her leaving so soon, and fills me with a hope for the future that I last felt with her, fifteen years earlier. "I love you so damn much," she breathes into my mouth, and I nip at her lower lip.

Lifting her in my arms, I move us toward my bedroom, kicking the door closed behind me. "Livvy won't be home from ballet for another hour." I'm unbuttoning my shirt as fast as my fingers let me.

"I know." She grins coyly, whipping her sweater over her head. Flicking open the top buttons of her jeans, my eyes zero in and she pauses. "Eyes up here, hot shot."

Chuckling, I force myself to look up, lingering on her breasts a moment too long because she clears her throat.

"Yes?" I ask, finally meeting her gaze.

"We're going to be okay, right?" Her face is open, vulnerable, and something inside of me shifts.

I give a solemn nod. "Me and you will always be okay. That's a promise, Lee."

"Promise," she repeats, raking her teeth over her bottom lip.

"Now get naked," I tell her, stepping out of my pants.

Everly's laughter rings out, musical. She tackles me onto my bed, straddling me. Reaching up, I cup her cheeks, staring into her beautiful, dazzling eyes, before sliding my hands down her shoulders and capturing her wrists. Tugging her forward, she collapses on my chest and I roll her beneath me. Slanting my mouth over hers, I kiss her until I'm drunk on her. I glide my lips over her neck, loving the way she squirms beneath me, desperate to hear the moans that fall from her mouth.

Some of her sweetness morphs into spice, and when I tug her earlobe in between my teeth, she hisses. Settling between her thighs, she arches into me, groaning as I pepper open-mouthed kisses down the column of her neck, moving lower. Gripping her hip, I kiss her stomach, memorizing the dips and curves of her body with my fingertips. Everly bucks against me as I dip my tongue into her belly button.

"Hold still, Lee." I chuckle, rubbing the scruff of my cheek across her lower abdomen, fascinated by the goosebumps that appear on her skin. "We're always in a rush, fumbling around in the dark, being quiet so Liv won't hear. I want to take my time with you, babe."

"Olivia is going to be home in an hour." She reminds me, a note of hysteria in her tone.

"I plan to spend it savoring you." I glance up, watching her eyes widen as I hook her thigh over my shoulder. "Let me take my time and enjoy this, Lee."

She shudders, dropping her head back and closing her eyes. Her hands grip my shoulders, her fingernails digging into my skin.

Pressing a kiss to her hipbone, I yank her underwear to one side. Desperate to taste her, I drop my head, my hands gripping her thighs, my thumb grazing over …

Everly flinches, and her entire body stiffens.

Frowning, I glide my thumb over the crease of her groin again. *What the fuck is that?* Confusion rocks through me as I peer at her soft skin, horrified by the three circles branded on her. Three perfect dots, the size of a pen cap…or a cigarette. My eyes jump to her opposite hip, noting the ridges of scars there.

"Everly?"

Leaning up on her elbows, she shakes her head, her hair falling over her shoulders. "Don't get distracted now." Her voice is playful, but her eyes are terrified, searing into mine with a desperation that causes my confusion to morph into fury.

And fear.

Who the fuck marked my beautiful girl?

Who hurt her?

Searching for signs I may have missed, I balance on my forearms, my eyes scanning her skin, looking for confirmation. For proof. This isn't the result of an accidental fall or a drunken run in with a doorframe.

These marks were intentional.

Someone did this to Everly.

Lifting my eyes to hers, she shrinks back against the pillows and I wince.

"Baby, don't be scared." I keep my voice soft, my words slow, even as wildfire spreads through my veins. "Who hurt you, love?"

She shakes her head and I bite the inside of my cheek, trying to control my anger, hold on to my goddamn sanity.

"Aaron, it was a long time ago, a misunderstanding." She scoots back on the bed until her back hits the headboard. Folding her knees into her chest, she wraps her arms around them and looks at him, pleadingly.

Fuck.

Sitting back until I'm kneeling on the bed next to her, I take her hand in mine and squeeze her fingers. "Don't lie to me, Lee. Not about this."

"I'm not." Her voice is small, her eyes trained on the wall in front of her.

She's lying. Blatantly, to my face.

Like Kate.

All the right words in the completely wrong tone.

Everly's shoulders roll forward and she dips her chin, desperate to disappear into herself.

I blow out an exhale, yanking on the back of my neck.

Everly isn't Kate. She's not lying to hurt me.

She's lying to protect herself.

She's scared.

Hiding out, is what she said to me the day of The Fringe.

"Lee, who hurt you?"

She flinches, her eyelids dropping, blocking the light of her eyes.

"Love, please. I'm here for you. Whatever you need. But if someone hurt you, baby, I need you to tell me." I shift closer, wrapping her tense frame in my arms and holding her against my chest.

We sit in silence for long minutes as Everly's body slowly relaxes.

And it's the hardest fucking thing I've ever done.

Because while I hold her and kiss the crown of her head and run my fingers along her arm, my muscles are coiled so goddamn tightly, they ache. My blood is running hot, my mind clouded with scenarios and possibilities and suspects.

Who the fuck hurt my girl?

When?

Has she told anyone?

Is she scared to tell me?

Was it a one-time thing or did he keep hurting her?

Deep down, I know it's Corey Hughes. I know it as surely as I know Olivia is my daughter and Finn is my brother. But I need to hear Everly say the words; I need her to tell me the truth.

"Everly." I whisper against her hair.

Immediately, her body tightens up, her shoulders tense, on alert.

"Aaron." Her voice is broken, reverberating through the space between us like an echo.

"Who hurt you?"

"I-I can't talk to you about this."

Closing my eyes, I drop my weight against the headboard, holding Everly tightly against my chest. "Can't or won't?"

"I-I'm not ready."

"Baby, please. Let me in."

She sighs, turning slowly to look at me.

And the pain in her eyes renders me speechless, turning some of my anger into devastation. For her. For what she lost. For what he took.

"I want to. I will. But, I'm not there yet. Please, Aaron. I need you to trust me. There are things, things I want to tell you, that I want to confide in someone about but I'm not, I can't." She shakes her head. "Not tonight. Olivia's coming home. We're going to have dinner and make a plan for while I'm on tour. Please, let me tell you when I'm ready. Don't force me."

Don't force me.

Those words, coming from her mouth, in that desperate, pleading voice, steals my retort from my throat. Dread spreads through me as guilt settles in my stomach. Her word choice is all wrong, implying horrors I hadn't even considered. "Baby, I'd never force you to do anything you don't want to do."

She nods, dropping her eyes and pulling the sheet tighter around her body.

"I love you, Everly. And I'm here for you. Always. Whatever you want to tell me, whenever you're ready to say it, I'm here."

"Thank you."

Sighing, I pull Everly closer. The silence wraps around us as we both travel in our own thoughts.

How do I prove to Everly that I'm here for her?

Is she really okay?

Who the hell put his hands on her?

What else did he do to her?

Do I possess enough patience to trust her the way she asked?

Why does she feel like she can't be honest with me?

Is this how the end started between Kate and me? An inability to communicate and trust each other?

No, but Everly asked you for time and understanding. She's still communicating.

Fuck. Why is everything always so goddamn difficult?

"Aaron, Olivia will be home in twenty minutes."

"Aye." I untangle myself from Everly. "Take a hot

shower, love. I'll fix dinner." Forcing myself to dress, I leave Everly alone and let my thoughts consume me.

Please, please, please, let us be okay.

THAT NIGHT, after Olivia is sleeping soundly and the kitchen is cleaned from our dinner, I pull the calendar up on my laptop, and Everly and I sit down at the kitchen table, ready to have the serious conversation we've been dancing around for weeks.

Except now, after earlier, it feels even more serious. Tension stretches between us like rubber bands, about to snap.

"We're doing this," Everly breathes out, her eyes drinking in the calendar like it's more than just a bunch of dates.

"We're doing this," I repeat, scanning the months. "If you want to."

"I do. Honestly, Aaron, I want this. I just, it's going to take me time to be forthcoming about certain things. Please, be patient with me."

Nodding, I yank on the back of my neck. "I'm trying, babe. I really am. Okay, what are your tour dates?"

Everly opens a document on her phone and begins rattling off cities and dates.

After nearly an hour, we've agreed Olivia and I will

fly out to see her Orlando performance, followed by a day at Disney World. I've also decided to catch her New York concerts at the end of January since it's an easy flight, and we always have Anderson business in Manhattan.

Additionally, Everly is going to visit me in Edinburgh during a break in her schedule in early March. Once things wrap for her in April, we're committed to finding a solution that works for both of our lives, both of our careers.

To be honest, it looks like she'll be spending more time in Scotland due to Olivia's school schedule, but once summer rolls around, Liv and I will be able to visit her in Tennessee. All in all, the planning went much smoother than expected. But I think that's because we were both desperate to avoid the elephant in the room. Well, Everly is avoiding it and I'm avoiding making her feel uncomfortable.

It's ironic really, that the conversation I've been nervous to have with her, the one that outlines our future, was so much easier than the conversation I'm now desperate for her to initiate.

When Everly gives me her body later that night, things between us feel different. There's a solemnity between us, a trust that is deeper than the physical. Like we've learned parts of each other's hearts as well as we memorized each other's bodies. We build a rhythm constructed from love. From the past, the present, and the future. From everything we have to give.

Tears shimmer in Everly's eyes as she presses her trust into my body, slowly but deliberately. In turn, I give her my patience, my understanding, my goddamn everything.

And it's so fucking beautiful and raw and real, I cling to it until dawn.

16
🎵 everly 🎤

N ow that my time in Edinburgh is coming to a
close, my impending farewell eats at me. My life
here seems to have evolved overnight, but I know it was
a slow progression of things. My relationship with
Aaron, slowly confiding in him and letting him see
pieces of me that I hide from everyone else is a game
changer. Because even though he doesn't know all my
truths, he suspects enough to know that the perception
of my dreamy, incredible life isn't always the reality I
lived.

Finding my confidence again, discovering my own
strength, and writing all the words for an incredibly
honest, soulful song reminded me how much I love my
passion when I'm not performing on demand. I've
finally found my footing here, in this city, in Aaron's
life, in my own future, and I don't want to say goodbye.

To drag out the days and make the most of my
moments, I've been spending nearly all of my free time
at Aaron's house, hanging with him and Olivia. I love

being pulled into their nightly routines, their morning rituals, and everything in between. On the days when Aaron is running behind at work and Olivia doesn't have extracurricular activities, I even pick her up from school. Sometimes, we stop for an ice cream or swing by Daisy and Finn's apartment.

Today, that's exactly where we are headed.

Mid-November is marked with a chill, the start of winter.

"You warm enough?" I ask Olivia, who nods, her chin tucked into her scarf.

By the time we make it to Daisy and Finn's, the cold has turned both of our noses red.

"It's too cold for this time of year," Daisy groans, pulling open the door to her apartment and taking in our winter gear. "I really do miss the Georgia sunshine."

"I hear ya, but don't you love cozy sweater weather?"

"Not as much as I did in January. Come on in." She holds the door open, and Olivia rushes from my side into the apartment. "Hey Liv."

"Hi Daisy!" Livvy calls over her shoulder, beelining to the basket of toys that Finn and Daisy keep for her.

"You're coming Friday, right?" Daisy asks me, pulling my hat off of my head.

"Absolutely. And thanks for tonight. Livvy is super excited to sleep over."

"It's all me. Finn's just in charge of building the forts and picking up the cake for breakfast." Daisy grins, her honey-brown hair bouncing in a high ponytail. "Come have a coffee."

Now that Daisy has moved past her stage of fangirling, which flattered the hell out of me, we've settled into an easy friendship. Two southern girls involved with two Scottish brothers: we get each other.

"How was your trip to the U.S.?" I ask, sliding onto a barstool at the kitchen island. Daisy flew to New York for a long weekend, accompanying Finn on a business trip, but really she went to see her brother, her best friend, and their sweet baby girl, Luna.

On the floor next to us, Olivia unpacks her My Little Ponies and begins to play. Daisy pops a coffee pod into the Nespresso machine on her countertop.

"It was amazing! Luna is my first niece, and I am so smitten with her. She's so sweet and cuddly and smells perfect." Daisy sighs. "Honestly, saying goodbye this time was so much harder. Especially because my brother and Sierra are considering a move back to the South."

"Really?"

She nods. "Milk and sugar?"

"Please."

Once Daisy hands me my coffee and begins preparing her own, she continues, "Yes, the last few years my three brothers all moved in different directions, but now they all seem to be migrating back home. Jax and his fiancé, Evie, have been in Texas, but she's wrapping up her studies in another year, and then I think they will go back to Georgia, too. My brother Carter never left, so…"

"It's just you who will be away."

She sighs. "I'm honestly fine with it. This is what I wanted. But it still makes me feel homesick sometimes."

"I know what you mean." I stir my coffee, my mind wandering to Addison and our boozy weekend brunches. Even though my friends in Nashville know nothing about my life with Corey, I still miss them. I think about the guys from the recording studio, the fantastic sisters, Ginger and Grace, who build out all of my branding, my stylists Kelly and Andre, who do my makeup and keep me on trend.

I left Nashville in such a hurry that I didn't say goodbye to anyone. But now that I've had time to settle, to gain a slice of clarity, there are pieces of me that miss my home.

"When are you heading back?" Daisy asks, sipping her coffee.

"In a week," I admit. "I'm supposed to start on my new tour in January, and I need to get back to rehearsals before then. There's a lot of preparations to be made, and I'm going to have to really work at it and commit to be ready in time. And, I was invited to perform at the Grand Ole Opry."

"Shut up!" Daisy grips my forearm. "That's huge."

"You're leaving next week?" Olivia interrupts, her voice accusing.

Turning toward her, the silent tears staining her cheeks drive a spike through my chest.

"Oh Livvy." I slide off my barstool, kneeling on the floor beside her, but she's backing away, shaking her head.

"No, you can't leave. You can't just leave!"

"Olivia." Daisy's voice is calm. "Everly has to go back to work. Her job is in America."

"Why can't she find a job here?" Olivia looks at Daisy. "You did."

"I know honey, but my type of job is different than Everly's."

Olivia swings her eyes back to me. "You made him happy again. You can't just leave. Why don't you want me?" She sobs harder and my heart cracks.

Little fissures expand the longer I take in her sobbing frame. Daisy scoops Olivia up into her arms and relocates them to the back bedroom.

Sitting in a state of shock, the pieces of my happiness begin to break off and crumble around me, like pieces of bark followed by branches from an apple tree. The fruit that once sustained me turns sour in the pit of my stomach. The little girl I once was, the one who was never enough for my own mother, sparks to life inside, as I fully understand Olivia's fears, her feelings, her doubts. They slam into me hard, physically knocking me back, as I try to reconcile what I know to be true: that Aaron and I can figure this out, that I didn't do anything wrong, that Olivia is entitled to her feelings, with what I know it means, that Aaron and I need to have another serious conversation.

"She's sleeping," Daisy whispers when she emerges from the bedroom. "Don't worry too much about Olivia. Aaron will speak to her and help her understand. I think she was just caught off guard on top of being very tired." She frowns. "I shouldn't have brought up your tour in front of her."

"It's okay." I try to smile, placing my coffee cup in the sink. "I should get going. Thanks for the coffee."

"Hey, you okay?" Daisy asks, her eyes scanning my face.

I nod, plastering on the mask I'm so good at hiding behind. "Of course. I just... I want to speak with Aaron to make sure he handles things with Olivia delicately. Thank you again for keeping her tonight."

"Sure, it's no problem."

"See you soon." I pick my purse up from the countertop and leave Daisy and Finn's apartment.

While my smile stays intact and I walk with measure, inside my blood turns to ice, as a winter frost begins to fill my veins. Slowly, reality seeps into the protective bubble I've been hiding in.

And I begin to numb myself to the pain that's undoubtedly coming.

Me: Hey Aaron. I just dropped Olivia at Finn and Daisy's. She heard me and Daisy talking about me leaving and is upset. I think you should head over there. Let's raincheck tonight.

Aaron: What happened?

Me: I think you should talk to her.

Aaron: I will. But I'm asking you.

Me: She doesn't want me to leave and asked why I can't find a job here. She was crying. I feel awful, Aaron.

Aaron: Don't. We will figure it out. I'll talk to her... I should have prepared her for this.

Me: Call me tomorrow.

Aaron: I'll see you later.

WATCHING RERUNS OF *THE OC*, I pour myself a tumbler with three fingers of whiskey and pull out the impressive stack of take-out menus I've accumulated in my time here. Thai or Italian? Big decisions happening in my life.

Except I do need to make some big decisions. Sure,

Aaron and I hammered out a plan for the upcoming year, with a handful of dates that we will be in the same place, at the same time, together. When I marked my calendar with little pink hearts for our days together, I was excited for the future. There was no doubt in my mind we could make this work.

But today, ugh, today changed everything.

Olivia's tears gutted me. Her sweet little face scrunched up, crying, begging me not to leave, felt like being punched in the throat. My bliss bubble popped, and I remembered exactly how it felt to be the little girl that no one wanted. Memories weigh on my conscience as I think about Olivia and the stability she needs.

Then, there's the painful awareness that I can't provide that. Sure, if I walked away from my career and relocated to Edinburgh, I'd be around for Aaron and Olivia. But I can't give up on myself, on my dreams, anymore. I've compromised too much in the past four years and while my career soared, it's now the only thing I have that truly belongs to me. I can't jeopardize my future or my independence to take a chance on a family, regardless of how desperately I want to belong to them.

A knock on the door startles me, and since I haven't placed a food order yet, I know it's Aaron.

"Hi," I greet him with hesitation, even though I want nothing more than for him to pull me into his arms and kiss me until I don't feel so empty, so guilty.

"Hey." He steps inside. "I brought food." He places two brown paper bags on the floor inside the door.

"Thai or Italian?"

"Thai."

I snort. "Good choice."

He offers me a smile, slipping out of his coat and hanging it on the coat rack. Placing his hands on either side of my face, he kisses me. "You okay, Lee?"

I nod, but my eyes well with traitorous tears at his sweetness, his gentleness. I made his daughter cry tears of anguish, and he still wants to know how I'm doing?

"What's going on?" he asks, taking my hand and pulling me to the couch in the living room.

I sit in the corner, tucking my knees up underneath me and hugging a pillow to my chest. "Aaron, I made Olivia cry."

"Because she adores you and is going to miss you."

"Because she needs a mother figure in her life and I- I don't know if it can be me. I don't live here. I'm leaving for the next six months at least. I—"

"You're putting way too much pressure on yourself. Olivia is my daughter, and as much as I want you to be a part of both of our lives, it's not your responsibility to alter your career or life to accommodate her needs. That's my job. I should have talked to her more about you, your career, our future. I should have included her more in decisions I was making that affect her life, too."

I sniffle, wiping the back of my hand across my nose. "I won't be that woman, Aaron."

"What woman are you referring to? Because I really love the woman I'm looking at."

Gah, this guy! Why is he so damn perfect? "I love you, too. And I love your daughter."

"I know you do."

"But a really long time ago, I was her. I watched the men flit in and out of my mother's life, and I clung to each of them like they could be my daddy, like if they loved me enough, they would stay. And it never happened. I don't want to disappoint her; I don't want to break her heart."

Aaron shifts on the couch, leaning forward and removing the pillow in my lap. Taking my hand in his, he brushes his thumb over my feather tattoo. "Everly, I don't know what's going to happen with us. Sure, you may end up disappointing Olivia at some point. But you know what? So will I. Let's just try to make those disappointments be things like buying the wrong ice cream flavor or forgetting to pack her ballet shoes for class."

I laugh in earnest.

"We can do this. I know we can. Today rattled you, and you have no idea how grateful I am to be with a woman who cares about my daughter's feelings as much as I do. But you don't need to feel guilty. You aren't that little girl anymore, and your mother and I are really different in the way that we parent, aren't we?" He raises his eyebrows and I nod.

Mom, while I loved her, never put me first. Over the

past few months with Aaron, I've always seen him make Olivia his top priority.

"Are you guys closer now that you're older?" he asks.

"She passed six years ago."

"Everly, I'm sorry." Aaron's voice dips and I shrug.

"Overdose. Caught me off-guard in the way sudden deaths do, but in reality I should have known it was coming."

Aaron shakes his head. "I thought, maybe with you becoming famous and—"

"That she would have been proud enough to quit?"

Aaron shrugs.

"Enough depressing chat." I stand from the couch, eyeing the takeout. "You sure Olivia is okay?"

"I'm positive." He reaches into his pocket and draws out a folded-up piece of construction paper. "I've been instructed to deliver this to you."

Grinning, I take the paper from his hands and open it. "She's the best," I say, viewing the drawing that Olivia made: a picture of Aaron, me, and her all smiling and eating ice cream cones.

"I told her you'd come see her tomorrow."

"Of course I will. Maybe we can go to the park if it doesn't rain."

"She'd love that."

"Me too."

"Come here." Aaron reaches out, tugging my hand until I fall back onto the couch. "I didn't even get to properly kiss you hello," he explains, his fingers curling around the nape of my neck and bringing my lips to his.

I'm so preoccupied with Aaron's kiss that I don't notice the messages lighting up my phone until hours later. And when I do, I wish I was still wrapped up in Aaron.

17

aaron

"Oh, Aaron Anderson, do I have a bone to pick with you," Daisy announces, walking into my office the next morning.

"No coffee this time?"

"I'm not as desperate for information this time."

I grin. "Then what are you here for?"

"To offer advice."

"Unsolicited."

"That's the best kind."

I gesture toward the chair across from my desk, and Daisy sits down, crossing her legs and studying me.

"Get on with it, Dais."

"You need to make a grand gesture."

"A what?" I lean forward, resting my elbows on my desk.

"You need to do something big for Everly. She's leaving in a week; you're not asking her to stay —"

"I can't ask her to stay. I told her I would never ask her to jeopardize her career, and that's exactly what I would be doing if I asked her that. We have a plan, we're going to figure the future out together, and on terms that work for both of us."

"Really? And does seeing her five times a year work for you?"

"What are you getting at, Dais?"

"What if you offer to go?"

"On tour?"

"To Tennessee."

Snorting, I shake my head and point to the framed photo of Olivia on my desk. "Olivia is my —"

"Entire world. And as she gets older, she's going to need a stronger, not to mention more reliable, mother figure in her life."

"Daisy. I appreciate you're looking out for me. I do. But I still don't have full custody of Olivia. I can't move her to America because I feel like it. Plus, I don't want to disrupt her stability, take her away from the only home and family and friends she's ever known."

Daisy nods, chewing her bottom lip. "True. I should have realized that. I just, I want you to be happy, Aar. Everly makes you happy and you guys are getting a second chance. Do you know how rare that is?"

"I do. That's why we're taking it seriously. And slowly. We're working something out that is beneficial for both of us."

"I get it. But a relationship isn't a business agree-ment, Aar. Feelings are involved and they tend to make everything…messy."

"I know. But right now, I can't offer a move to

America and I'm not asking her to stay. Any other grand ideas?"

Daisy sighs, standing up. "No, but if I think of something else, I'll be back."

"I have no doubt."

"Don't tell Finn I popped in about this. Tell him we were discussing the McKinnon account or something."

"He's warned you about meddling again?"

"He just doesn't have the same degree of emotional intelligence that I possess."

Chuckling, I nod. "I'll give you that."

"See you later, Aar." Daisy closes my office door.

Raising my water bottle to my lips, I take a long sip, thinking about Daisy's point.

Does Everly know how much I love her?

"She was giving you her opinion again, wasn't she?" My brother arrives in my office, drops into a chair, and slides a coffee, a real one from the coffee shop downstairs, onto my desk.

"You, at least, come bearing gifts."

"She needs to let it go. Whatever is between you and Everly, is between you guys."

"I agree." I take a sip of the coffee. "Too bad you didn't spike it."

"One of those days?"

I shrug. "As much as I don't want to admit it, on some level, I think Daisy is right. Maybe I need to be more forthcoming with Everly, offer her more of a reason to want to make a real future with me. She's had a tough relationship with her ex, and I don't know, I feel like maybe she doesn't know how much I love her. How much I want to create a real future, a family, with her."

"Ah, commitment issues. That's a new one," Finn remarks dryly. "Mate, give her some time. You're offering her as much as you can at the moment and were honest with her from the start. She was also honest with you, and I think if you asked her to stay, she just might say yes and end up resenting the hell out of you later. If you offer to go right now, it could mess things up for Liv and then put too much pressure on your relationship with Everly. These things take time."

"Aye." I concede the point.

"Anyway," Finn says, standing and stretching his legs, "don't let Daisy get in your head. She means well, and I love the hell out of her, but she's bloody nosy."

"Or she's just trying to recruit another Southern girl into the Anderson clan."

"Or that. Want to grab a pint at Reid's after work?"

"Sure. Let me just double check that Aunt Jenni can pick Livvy up from her ballet class."

"Okay. See you later."

Once he leaves, I confirm with Aunt Jenni, who offers to keep Olivia overnight.

Gripping the sides of my head, I turn back to the logos I'm looking at, trying to get my head back in the game. But all I can think about are Everly's dazzling green eyes.

> **Me:** Hey Lee, I'm grabbing a pint with Finn after work. Swing by after?

After twenty minutes with no response, I frown.

> **Me:** All okay? I'll pass by around seven.

> **Everly:** Hey. Not feeling well. I'm going home now to crash. Talk tomorrow?

> **Me:** Are you okay? I'll bring you some soup.

> **Everly:** Probably a bug. Call you tomorrow.

Frowning at the message, I call Everly, but it goes to voicemail. Something is wrong. I can sense it in the tone of her messages.

Mate, calm down. Maybe she really just doesn't feel well and isn't up for chatting.

But it's more than that. Her exchange with Olivia earlier in the week rattled her more than I thought it would.

Is she freaking out?

Is the future too complicated for her to want to try?

Are Olivia and I not enough for her? Or worse, too much?

Shutting down my computer for the day, I send Finn a message.

Right now, I really need that pint at Reid's before I drive myself crazy.

Except I'm already halfway there.

"Two pints, Deuchars IPA," Finn orders from our server.

"Add two shots of tequila," I tack on for good measure.

Finn chuckles but he doesn't comment.

As usual, Reid's Row bustles with the after-work crowd. Live music picks up shortly after Finn and I sit down, drowning out a lot of the conversations surrounding us, and providing a backdrop of noise to distract my mind from the thoughts ricocheting around my brain.

Pinching the bridge of my nose to lessen the ache in my head, I open my eyes to see my brother's concerned frown.

"What?" I ask him.

"You tell me. You were fine an hour ago."

"An hour ago, I wasn't contemplating the future of my relationship with Everly."

"What changed?"

"I don't know."

"You're not making any sense."

"I have a feeling," I say, trying to articulate the

uneasiness spreading through my limbs, causing a sickness to sweep through my stomach. "I feel... unsettled. The way I did when I knew something was up with Kate but couldn't put my finger on what it is."

"I'm going to kill Daisy."

I shake my head. "It's not her."

"Mate, Everly isn't cheating on you."

"But something is off." I nod my thanks to the server, picking up my shot glass and tossing it back. Staring at Finn's, I drink his, too.

He gestures for two more shots.

"What's off?" my brother asks, taking a pull of his beer.

"She's really torn up about Livvy and how her career and the distance will affect her."

"That's a good thing, isn't it? Being with a woman who cares about your kid?"

"Aye. Of course it is, but it's more than that. It's like she's questioning if she can do this. She has—had—a complicated relationship with her mum, and she knows what it's like to be the kid with the mum who dates around."

"But you're not dating around. Aar, we had to push you to go out for a coffee by yourself."

"I know. But Everly doesn't know that. In her head, she's the woman taking me away from Olivia, causing uncertainty in her life, making waves. And she remembers what it felt like to be that kid."

"I get that, but can't you talk to her about it?"

"I did."

"And?"

"She's rattled. It's as if she's torn between me and Olivia and her career. But, I thought she was fine after we talked. I don't know, Finn. Today, she's telling me she doesn't feel well and will talk to me tomorrow."

"Maybe she doesn't feel well," my brother says, looking at me like I'm losing my mind.

"Something's off, Finn. I can feel it. There have been too many things that just don't add up." Her words the day at The Fringe, the doctor at the ER, the scars on her hip and thigh, the way she's not ready to confide in me. She's dealing with something sinister and if it's what I suspect it is, I'm not sure how to help her from a damn prison cell after I murder Corey Hughes.

"You know what I think?"

"What?"

"I think you should take this shot." He passes me one of the shooters as the server hands them both to him. "And relax a little. Your life has been crazy over the past year, and you've barely had time to just sit and relax. Mate, things are good right now. Kate's out of your life, she hasn't been fighting you on Olivia and custody, and you're dating a beautiful, talented woman who makes you happy. Did you ever think you're just looking for issues because of everything that went down with Kate?"

"What do you mean?" I take the shot, hissing as the tequila burns the back of my throat.

"Your marriage fell apart because your wife—"

"Ex-wife."

"Ex-wife was cheating. Now, she's moved on and is gallivanting across Europe with her painter—"

"Musician."

"Whatever. Aaron, you're being paranoid, looking for holes, because you don't want to be blindsided again. You don't want the other shoe to drop when things are going so well. I think you're too damn scared to be happy, so you're looking for reasons not to be."

Squinting at my brother, I see he really believes what he's saying. It's written in the concern shadowing his expression.

"I don't know." I scrub a hand over my face.

"Enjoy your beer, Aaron. Hang for a bit. And if you're that worried about Everly, swing by her place and check in on her. But sometimes, things are exactly as they seem. She could just have a bug and be tired."

"I guess." Picking up my beer, I take a long pull, glancing around the pub. But even the pale ale doesn't ease the tightness in my chest.

18

🎵 everly 🎤

> Corey: Found you. Did you think you could elude me forever, Everly? I'm lost without you. Come home.

Rereading the series of messages flooding my inbox from Corey, my blood turns cold and floaters appear in my line of vision. It doesn't matter that I've had twelve hours to digest his words; they still make me sick to my stomach.

And the images. The images are the worst part. Dread weighs down my limbs and causes me to stay frozen in my apartment, fearful to step outside.

Since I first read Corey's message last night after Aaron left, I've barely ate, slept, or blinked. I'm paralyzed with fear that strikes at me harder since I didn't anticipate it. Sure, deep down, in my heart of hearts, I surmised that Corey was up to something.

But the blow blindsided me.

Thumbing through the messages and images Corey sent, I swallow back the bile that rises in my throat.

An image of me, laughing, my body language care-

free and natural, as I lean over a cafe table and brush crumbs off of Aaron's mouth. He's grinning at me, his blond hair bright in the sunshine. We look like the perfect couple. We look like we're... in love with each other.

Me from behind, pressed against the floor-to-ceiling windows in Aaron's apartment. I'm clad in black lingerie, my legs hooked around Aaron's waist, as he grips my hair and gazes at me with longing.

The two of us, kissing passionately, on Leith's Docks.

Aaron, Olivia, and me eating ice cream at our favorite shop in Stockbridge.

Corey knows.

A pit forms in my stomach, expanding outward until I can't breathe. Tossing down the phone like it burned me, I drop to my knees. Hanging my head forward, I drag small wisps of air into my lungs, but I can't hold onto them. I can't grab at them quickly enough.

Tears prick the corner of my eyes, cause my nose to burn, and my throat to ache.

Corey found me. He knows. He knows. He knows.

About Aaron.

About Olivia.

Oh my God, they're not safe.

I'm not safe.

I need to tell Aaron. I need to warn him.

The cold tile of my kitchen floor bites into my knees

as I crawl several paces and snatch my phone back up from where I dropped it.

Deep breath in. Count to five. Exhale.

Sitting back on my heels, I open my eyes and force myself to reread his messages, diving deeper into Corey's twisted mind.

> Corey: I forgot how sexy you are in lingerie.

> Corey: I thought strawberry was your favorite flavor?

> Corey: I miss you, baby. Even though you stuck a knife through my heart, I miss you.

> Corey: I want you back. And we both know, I always get what I want.

And the message that caused me to hyperventilate sent just an hour ago:

> Corey: Not heading out today? But I can't wait to see what you're wearing.

Jesus.

He's had me followed.

He's hired someone to spy on me.

He's spying on me right now.

Right this minute.

All the curtains in my apartment have been drawn for the entire day as I've sat here, in the dark, alone.

A noise sounds out, and even though I know it's the

refrigerator, my eyes dart around the kitchen, petrified that I'm going to come face to face with a camera lens.

Or Corey.

A shiver rolls through my body, violent in its intensity.

My phone beeps again and I cringe, fearful to read the message and fearful to ignore it. Steeling my back, I draw in a deep breath and glance at the screen.

"Oh God!" My hand lifts to cover my mouth as I squeeze my eyes closed.

But the image of Olivia in her pink tutu and ballet shoes, her hair pulled back into a neat bun, is burned into my eyelids. He knows where she is. Right this very moment.

And he's throwing down the ultimatum.

He's threatening me in a way he knows I'll react.

He's threatening Olivia.

I need to tell Aaron.

But he can't come here. I can't be with him.

He's in danger. Olivia is in danger.

Oh God, what am I going to do?

> Corey: Come home to me, Everly. I'm waiting for you.

A KNOCK on the door has me hiding in my kitchen, a knife in hand.

He's here. Corey is here. He's come to take me back.

"Everly? It's me." Aaron's voice on the other side of the door fills me with relief so sharp, it stabs me in the chest. Dropping the knife in the kitchen sink, I run to the door, pulling it wide open in fear that Corey will see him.

Surprise blooms on his face as I reach out and yank him into my apartment, flipping the lock behind him and adding the chain link.

"Woah," he says slowly, his eyebrows pulled low over his eyes. Teetering on his feet, he places both hands on my shoulders, steadying himself and peering into my eyes. "How do you feel? Is it a stomach bug?" His brogue is thicker than usual, his pupils dilated.

The tequila from his breath washes over my face, and I shuffle back a step.

"Hey, what's wrong? Baby, talk to me."

Baby, talk to me.

"Baby, talk to me. I didn't mean it, Everly. Come on." He pounds the bathroom door with the butt of his fist, but I know better than to be fooled by his kind words.

There is nothing kind about Corey Hughes when he's been drinking.

Huddled in the corner of the bathroom, my knees pulled into my chest, I drop my forehead onto my kneecaps and sit. Paralyzed. Numb.

Numb except for the burning that mars the right side of my ribs, the blood trickling down my side and sopping into the band of my underwear.

He cut me. With a knife.

Sure, he didn't mean to. He told me we were just playing a little game. One where I wasn't supposed to move.

Except I did move. That's why the knife sliced through me.

Because I moved.

And I wasn't supposed to.

I broke the rule.

I broke his rule.

And he had no choice but to follow through with the consequences.

It's my fault.

If I hadn't been so flirty with Ben Links at the label's party tonight, we wouldn't have had to play the game.

Corey only likes to play games when I make mistakes. When I break the rules.

And tonight, I broke the rules. I had too much to drink. One glass of champagne too much. I was dressed too seductively, in a red dress that drew too much attention.

"Baby, talk to me." His words are sharper now, his tone harder.

I wiggle my ass against the tiles, and the right side of my body blazes with fire.

Deep breath in. Count to five. Exhale.

"Baby, open the door. We can fix this. I need you, Everly. Please, let me make this right." "Lee?" Aaron's hands squeeze my shoulders as he bends, peering into my eyes.

Blinking, I glance up at him, watching as the amusement in his eyes fades, his expression turning grave. He sobers instantly, his playful tipsiness forgotten.

"Aaron, we need to talk." I shuffle back a step, but he follows.

"Everly." He pulls me against his chest and wraps his arms around me. One hand snakes up my back, his long fingers disappearing into my hair as he cradles my head. "Lee, I know it's a lot. And I know you're scared about leaving next week, about me and Olivia, but we're going to figure this out. We should have talked sooner. I don't even know how you feel about being a mother figure in Liv's life. Did I expect too much too soon? Tell me, Lee. What's going on?"

Gripping the cloth of his shirt in my fists, I drop my forehead against his chest and inhale a shaky breath. The air feels like icicles stabbing my throat as goose-bumps prickle my skin.

I need to tell him the truth. I need to come clean. I need to be honest and lay my soul so bare, I hope I'm still standing at the end. I hope he's still holding me when I'm finished.

"Aaron, I'm in trouble."

Aaron's body stiffens under my touch as he shuffles

back. His eyebrows draw down, his blue eyes blazing, both glacial and melting. "Lee?"

"We should sit down."

"Baby, are you okay? What kind of trouble?"

"The worst kind."

Aaron guides me to the couch and we both sit. His foot taps against the floor in impatience, his shoulders rigid. "Tell me, Everly. Tell me everything."

My hands shake as I tuck strands of hair behind my ears. Looking around the room, my eyes settle on my phone and I resign myself to being truthful. "Corey and I didn't really break up, not the way most people do."

"What? You're —"

"I ran away."

"Everly?"

"Aaron, please. I've never told anyone, except Addison, about this before. Please just let me get it out." I glance up at him and he nods, his expression equal parts horror and fury. His jaw ticks with tension, his hands balled into fists.

"I met Corey at a party for my label when I was twenty-six. He was charismatic and charming. The kind of guy who walked into any room and owned it. At the time, I found him extremely impressive. He knew all the right people, said all the right things, and was always in high demand. He could make someone a country star. And he could tear them down just as easily. The first time we met, I don't think I even landed on his radar. But as my career flourished and my songs became more popular, he began taking note of me at label events and different Nashville functions. He would comment on a new single or music video, compliment me on the lyrics of a song, offer tidbits of advice that I soaked up. Being noticed by him was a high. He was the guy every artist wanted to know, and he looked at me like he really saw me." I pause, tears welling in my eyes. Aaron moves closer, his hand finding mine. God, how stupid and naïve I was. But back then, my life seemed so simple, so damn sunny.

"He asked me out at my thirtieth birthday party. It was a huge event with a lavish cake and a celebrity-studded guest list. Addison had planned it and she spared no expense. When Corey asked me to dinner, I was giddy to say yes. Our relationship moved pretty quickly after our first date. Within a few months, we were living together, being photographed around town, blowing up on social media. My career soared; my album sales skyrocketed. Corey began advising on my new album, consulting with my team regarding my appearance, scheduling different media opportunities for me. In short, he began stepping on Addison's toes and she hated it. It put a huge strain on our friendship, but I didn't know what to do. I thought I was in love with Corey and it's almost like I couldn't hear anyone except him. For nearly two years, everything seemed great. Perfect, even. I hit the *Billboard* charts and performed a sold-out tour. I was on the cover of magazines and did big-name interviews. And I was on the arm of Corey Hughes."

Aaron's hand tightens on my fingers, his jaw clenching. His eyes burn with anger, with a hate I've never witnessed in their depths before. "Go on."

"The first time he hit me, I was more shocked than angry. Isn't that messed up? I instantly felt guilty for making him angry. He was furious about a dress I wore to an event and a man, a fellow country artist, who commented on how pretty I looked. It was stupid. But his reaction, to smack me across the face after we got home and I was pulling bobby pins from my hair, seemed irrational. The next morning, he was so apologetic. He cried as he held me against his chest and apologized over and over again, telling me about how stressed out he was, about how overwhelming things were at the moment. And I felt guilty. I felt bad for him. How fucked up is that?"

Aaron looks away, hiding the expression on his face. But his body lurches in response to my words, his muscles coiled so tightly, he seems to vibrate in his fury. "The first time?"

"Things deteriorated from there."

"How many times did he fucking hit you, Lee? How many times did that bastard put his fucking hands on you?" He turns, his expression violent, his eyes midnight blue, streaked with anger.

"Too many." I whisper.

Aaron sighs, closing his eyes. His hand leaves mine as he buries his face in his palms, his shoulders shaking with emotion. "Why didn't you tell anyone?"

"Addison knows. She found me one night, crying in the bathroom. She took one look at me, cursed, turned around and ripped into Corey. I have no idea what she said to him but after that night, he eased off a bit and Addison slowly took back the ground she lost in managing my career."

"Why would he be intimidated by Addison?"

"She's probably the only person in Nashville with better connections and more financial backing then him. She comes from an Old Southern family with Old Southern money, the kind that not many people can boast these days."

"Lee, why didn't you tell the police?"

"I couldn't tell the police."

"Why not?"

"Are you crazy? It would destroy my career; it would ruin the only thing I have left."

"The only thing you have left?" Hurt causes Aaron's voice to waver and I sigh, my stomach plunging to my toes.

"Aaron, please. I didn't mean it like that. It's just, I've worked really, really hard for my career. For my success. And Corey manipulates it all. He always has. If I go to the authorities, he'll try to ruin me. The scandal of it all will ruin me. I'll no longer be 'Everly Pierce, country sweetheart.' I'll be 'Everly Pierce, battered victim, stupid girl who stayed with the wrong guy when she knew better.' People will pity me, and I can't stand that judgement. I can't live through it. No one understand what my life was like. And I don't want anyone to."

"Everly, he hit you."

"It's my fault." I respond automatically.

"Baby, no." Pain blooms in Aaron's expression, his eyes taking on a new shade of agony.

"You don't know him like I do. You don't know what he's capable of. The last time he beat me, I thought it was the end. I thought he was going to kill me. And instead of confronting him or asking for help, I ran away. I hid out and healed and then I came here. And now, he knows. He sent me this." I swipe my phone off the table and hand it out to Aaron.

He glances down at the photo of Olivia, his eyes snapping up to mine. "What the fuck, Lee? Is he here?" Aaron pulls his cell out of his pocket, pressing a button and holding it to his ear. "Aunt Jenni? You have Liv? Is she okay?" His words trip over each other before he exhales, his body slumping forward. "Aye. Please, just keep her inside with you and Uncle James. I'll be by to pick her up in a bit and we'll talk then. Thank you. 'Bye." He ends the call, his eyes latching onto mine once more. "Why the fuck does he know who my daughter is?"

Tears prick my eyes, gathering in the corners no matter how quickly I blink. "It's a threat."

Aaron stands, springing from the couch and walking toward the closed blinds on my windows. "Everly —"

"I'm going back to Nashville, Aaron."

Aaron turns, stumbling back as though I physically shoved him. "Not to him, you're not."

"He won't touch Olivia. Or you."

Chuckling humorlessly, Aaron's eyes swing wildly around my apartment. "You're damn right he won't. But not because you're sacrificing yourself to him. Stop with the fucking martyr shit. Me and you, we're in every goddamn thing together. I'm sorry if I didn't make that clear before but I'm not giving up on us, Everly. I'm not letting you go again. And I'm definitely not going to sit back and watch while you run back to him." Aaron's voice drops, deceptively soft while his body vibrates with outrage.

"It's a game. And I have to play by the rules." I squeeze my palms between my thighs and close my eyes. *You know the rules, Everly. You know what you need to do.* Corey's voice breathes in my mind. *There are always consequences when you break the rules.*

"What? You're not making any goddamn sense." Aaron grips at his hair.

"You don't know him like I do. I need to go back. I need to end things between us for real. I can't hide away forever, always scared he's going to appear, worried about every text and email I get. I can't keep living this half-life. I need to do what I should have done years ago. And I need you and Olivia safe."

"Everly, I can take care of myself and Olivia. And you. This guy —"

"Is my problem to handle."

"Like you've been handling it the past four years?" Aaron spews, shaking his head and pinching the bridge of his nose. "Fuck. Fuck, Everly, I'm sorry. I'm so fucking —"

"I know." I breathe out, wiping a hand over my cheek. "You're scared."

"I'm livid."

"With me?" I whisper.

Immediately, Aaron's eyes soften, and he closes the space between us in three strides. Dropping to his knees in front of the couch, he takes my hands in his and tugs me forward. "God, baby, never with you. With him. With myself. How did I miss this, Lee? How did I miss all the signs? You dropped hints baby, and I brushed them aside. And this whole damn time you've been suffering in silence. I haven't been here for you the way I should have. But I am now. And I'm not letting you walk out of here and go back to him. I've got us, and I've got Olivia. Do you understand me? We will figure this out."

"We can't involve the police." I shudder at the thought, imagining the headlines and social media memes. Picturing my ruined career, the mud Corey would drag my reputation through, colors my reality even bleaker than it is.

"Everly —"

"Aaron, please —"

The ringing of his phone cuts through the air, silencing us both. He answers it quickly, anxiety stamped into his expression. "Aunt Jenni? What's wrong?" Aaron's face drops, his mouth twisting as he listens to his aunt. "How high? Did you give her paracetamol? Aye, of course. I'm on my way." He hangs up the phone and exhales. "Olivia spiked a fever. Aunt Jenni is worried and Liv's asking for me."

"Go."

He eyes me warily. "I hate leaving you like this, Lee. Come with me."

"No," I shake my head, my mind shutting down from the emotionally overwhelming day. "Liv needs you, Aaron. Go be with your daughter."

"We're not done with this conversation, Everly. I'll come by tomorrow before work. We'll get breakfast and finish talking this through, okay, baby?"

I nod.

"We're in this together, Lee. I'm here for you." He cups my cheek, his hand warm even though it feels like my face is on fire. "I love you, baby. I'll always love you and nothing will ever change that. You're a goddamn warrior, so don't think of yourself as anything less."

"Okay."

"See you in the morning."

I nod, brushing my lips across his when he leans forward. Walking Aaron to the door, I fall into his arms for one last hug. Once he's gone and the chain link is intact, I pull out my suitcases and dial my lifeline. She answers on the third ring. "Addi, it's me."

19

aaron

"Daddy's here, little love." I trail my hand over Liv's sweaty hair as she groans in her sleep. My baby's fever is too high, and a different kind of fear grips my chest.

"I gave her paracetamol an hour ago." Aunt Jenni fusses at the foot of Olivia's bed. "Her fever should be coming down by now." She turns to the dresser and opens a drawer, pulling out a fresh set of sheets. "She's sweating and not drinking nearly enough water."

"Jesus." Taking in Olivia's tiny frame, I reach for her water cup on the bedside table when her body begins to shake. Uncontrollably. "Olivia." I lurch forward, grabbing onto one of her legs while my daughter's body convulses, her eyes rolling back in her head. "Olivia!"

"She's having a seizure." Aunt Jenni rushes to the bedroom door and flings it open. "James! Call 9-9-9!" She calls out the UK's emergency services number. "Don't move her, Aaron. It should stop in a few moments."

Dropping to my knees, I turn Liv onto her side and cling to her, feeling helpless. "Daddy's here, baby. You're okay, Liv. Stay with me. Daddy's here." I murmur nonsensical nothings, mentally pleading for the seizure to stop.

"Ambulance is on its way." Uncle James barrels into the room.

"It's stopped." I say, tears falling over my eyelids as Olivia's body stills and then stirs awake.

"Daddy?"

"I'm right here, little love. Right here."

"It was just over two minutes long." Aunt Jenni whispers to Uncle James, shouldering Olivia's overnight bag.

Sirens sound in the distance.

"Lift her gently, Aaron, and bundle her in the comforter. We need to go to the hospital." Aunt Jenni's voice is quiet but strong.

Tucking the blanket around Olivia, I cradle her against my chest, breathing in her sweet scent and watching her eyelashes flutter.

"I'll follow you in the car." Uncle James says, holding the bedroom door for us.

"Thank you. Aunt Jenni, would you ride with us?"

"Of course, dear."

"Uncle James, please, call Kate?"

"I will. See you at the hospital." My uncle is already pressing buttons on his phone.

"It's okay, little love. Daddy's got you. We're just going to make sure you're okay now."

"Love you, Daddy." Liv's voice breathes out, sweet and soft.

"I love you all the world, Livvy."

"I DIDN'T KNOW she missed a vaccine. Of course I would have taken her." The excuses fall from Kate's mouth like raindrops. Effortlessly and without care for who they affect.

Right now, they're falling on deaf ears.

Because I don't care. I don't care about her excuses. I don't care about her reasoning.

"Kate, we fucked up."

"Aaron, please, it was an honest mistake. Olivia —"

"Is lying in a hospital bed with meningitis."

"I know." Kate sighs, her mouth falling slack. "I had no idea missing the polio vaccine could—"

"I don't care."

"Excuse me?"

"I don't fucking care what the reasons are. We failed our daughter. Don't you understand? We messed up. For the past however many months you've been gallivanting around, she hasn't been our number one priority."

"I've been gallivanting around? What about you,

Dad of the Year? What about all of those months where you barely made it home in time to kiss her goodnight?"

"Aye, I wasn't always the best father. I'll admit it. But you've barely been a mother at all lately. It's bad enough you had to ruin our family, but to put our daughter's health in jeopardy —"

"Why haven't you been following the immunization schedule?" Kate jabs a finger into my chest, and I glance down, sneering at the bright red varnish on her nails.

"It's been a lot lately, Kate. Changing my work schedule, picking up your slack—"

"Slack! Is that what you call the first six years of Livvy's life when you were too busy being a workaholic to remember you had a family?"

"I was providing—"

"Save it. You're as much to blame as I am for this."

"Fine. Do you feel better now, appropriating blame? Poor Kate, the martyr, the victim, the bored housewife that needed her career back to define her. You —"

"Fuck you, Aaron."

Groaning, I drop my head back. *Why am I allowing this to spin out of control? Why am I engaging in conversation at all with Kate that isn't centered on Olivia?* "We failed her, Kate."

Kate sighs, dropping back into her hospital chair. "I know."

"What do you want to do?" I sit in the chair next to her. Taking in her profile, the column of her neck, the beauty mark next to her right eyebrow, the diamond earrings I bought her for our five-year anniversary, I hardly recognize her. I can draw every detail of Kate's face with my eyes closed, and yet staring at her now is like looking at a stranger. A wariness I don't recognize ripples over her features, a desperation I don't understand flashes in her eyes when she meets my gaze.

"I'd like to sign over full custody to you."

"What?"

Tears twist Kate's features, as she swipes a hand across her face. "You're right, I messed up and—"

"Kate, stop. We both made mistakes. But you're Olivia's mother. You'll always be her mother."

"I know. You're right. But right now, I don't think I can give her everything she needs. Not like you can. I don't want to keep lying to her Aaron or to myself. Right now, the best place for me is in Spain with Paul."

The flicker of empathy I felt toward Kate moments ago dies a sudden death. In its place, a burning anger, borderline rage, consumes me. "Are you fucking kidding me? You're going to sign your parental rights over to me, just like that? We're not talking about a puppy. Olivia is our daughter."

"This is hard enough of a decision for me without you piling on the guilt." Kate looks up, her eyes glinting with an edge that aches more than it cuts.

"It doesn't seem that way," I say quietly. If I speak louder, the rage eating at me may come roaring out, decimating the entire hospital. "Do you know how this is going to hurt Olivia? How this will affect her?"

"Then don't tell her. Just tell her I'll see her for Christmas." Kate stands from her hospital chair. "I'm going to get a coffee."

I stare, literally gaping at the woman I once called my wife. I don't even recognize Kate which isn't a surprise since I haven't seen the woman I fell in love with in a long, long time. Kate's re-entrance into the workforce eighteen months ago changed everything in our marriage, in our family. She "found herself" again. And apparently that trumped parenting.

"She's always been a piece of work." Finn comments, handing me a cup of coffee. He places a third down by the leg of his chair. "I grabbed her one, but I think she needed a moment."

"She was never like this."

"Aye. She's changed. Mid-life crises?"

"Fuck if I know. Olivia used to be her world but now, everything is about Paul. She wants to sign over parental rights."

"What?" Finn's mouth drops open. "Are you sure?"

Shrugging, I sip the coffee. "I just want my daughter to be okay, Finn. I don't have the energy to try to figure out where Kate's head is at. Or Everly's. I can't, I can't even think about where I think she is right now because I'll spiral. And right now, I need to be here, show up, for my daughter."

"Where would Everly be? Did you get into a fight?"

"We had a conversation last night, one we started and never finished. I was supposed to pick her up for breakfast today so we could talk but she's not answering my calls or responding to my messages so…"

"So?"

"I think she flew back to Tennessee."

"When Liv's sick?"

"She doesn't know it's meningitis. Just that Liv had a fever last night. I'm worried about her, Finn."

"Liv or Everly?"

"Both. I'm so goddamned worried I feel sick."

"I'll swing by Everly's flat to check in on her. What's going on, Aar?"

Hanging my head, I close my eyes, trying to sort out my own jumbled thoughts and quell the rage burning me from the inside out. My daughter has meningitis. I fucked up. Corey hurt Everly. He put his hands on her and marked her and broke her heart and probably a hell of a lot more than I even know.

Kate wants to live in Spain with a musician she's known for a year instead of raising her daughter. *When the hell did that happen? How could I have fucked up so many things, not seen what the hell was really happening, in such a short amount of time?*

"Aaron?" Finn prompts.

"She's hurt."

"Who?"

"Everly."

"What happened?"

"He's going to hurt her again."

"Aar, start at the beginning."

Dropping my head back, I stare at his ceiling. "Things between Everly and me developed quickly."

"Aye. Just a few months. But that's more likely when you have a history, which you guys do, and when you're older."

I narrow my gaze and he shrugs. "I'm not being a bawbag about it. When you're in your thirties, you usually know more about what you want in a partner and the type of lifestyle you're looking for than when you're twenty-five."

"I guess. Things escalated quickly, and aye, we have history. But there have been several, I don't know, moments, when I felt like I was missing an important piece of the puzzle. Like there was something important I wasn't seeing. Or, fuck, I was seeing it but not admitting what the hell it all meant."

"Is this about what I said at the pub? Are you pissed because of what I said about Kate?"

"No, I'm pissed because I didn't trust my gut the way I should have. And now, Everly's running back to him because she's scared for me and Liv."

"To who?" my brother practically growls.

"Her ex-boyfriend." I force myself to look at my brother. "He hurts her, Finn."

Since I'm staring right at him, I see as the confusion in his eyes fades to surprise and then flickers with unbridled fury. "No fucking way."

Rolling my shoulders forward, my left knee bounces up and down, and it's all I can do to stay seated, to tell Finn everything I know. "That first day, when I saw her at The Fringe, she said she was here 'hiding out.'" I quote her words. "And we laughed it off. But then, at the hospital, the doctor wanted to speak to her privately about her X-rays and left her his card." I pause, other memories, moments that caused me a flicker of unease, come rushing back. "There have been times when she was jumpy, jittery. She's got these fucking scars…" I shudder, digging my fingers into my eyes to try to erase the image of burn marks on Everly's inner thigh.

Why didn't I press her harder to confide in me that night? Why did I wait?

Because she asked you to trust her.

But doesn't trusting her also mean recognizing when she needs me to be more than a comforting presence? To know when she's not okay?

"What?" Finn asks, his teeth clenched.

"There are marks on her inner thigh. Like a fucking cigarette. He burned her, Finn. And now, she's gone."

"Are you sure? I'm going to go by her flat, mate. I promise."

Tapping my head against the wall behind me, I nod. "She's gone back to Nashville."

"And now you can't leave."

"My number one priority is my daughter. It always will be."

20
🎵 everly 🎤

Landing at Nashville International Airport, I feel dead inside. Not just numb, but like a corpse. I know he's waiting for me, and I know I need to pull myself together before I step off the plane, but on the inside I have nothing left to give.

The horror in Aaron's eyes when I admitted, out loud, that I let Corey hit me chafes against my memory, causing shame to line my stomach. And then he offered to handle everything with me, to make decisions together. He truly believed that we could take on Corey Hughes and somehow win. The corners of my mouth turn up at the thought.

But I know better than to believe in miracles.

Corey Hughes always wins.

And he destroys everything and everyone on his path to victory.

Glancing at my phone, I leave it turned off. The truth is any messages from Aaron will scrape at my fresh heartache and the lack of any messages will hurt just as badly. Either way, I lose.

Ducking into the first-class bathroom before I exit the plane, I pull out my makeup bag and fix my face. Puffy from crying, pale from heartbreak, I look awful. But as luck would have it, I'm a master with a makeup brush, and I quickly transform myself into Nashville's own sunny and free-spirited Everly Pierce. Slipping studs into my ears, clasping my signature strands of beads around my neck, and donning a boho chic sweater that falls off one-shoulder, I look like any other woman after an international flight, tired but not depressed.

Cheers to small miracles.

Shouldering my bag, I take a deep breath and exit the aircraft, grinning at the people I pass on my way to baggage claim.

"Oh my God! Everly Pierce, we love you!"

"Is that Everly Pierce?"

"Her single, 'Mending Broken,' is everything."

"She looks so skinny. Do you think she does yoga?"

Entering baggage claim, my eyes spot him immediately.

Where the hell is Addison?

Standing front and center, with a few paparazzi bumbling about, Corey's holding a sign that reads "welcome home love." My heart sinks because the "love" is a dig at Aaron. He's going to make me pay.

His eyes meet mine and spark to life, a malicious twist to his mouth.

He's going to make me pay, and he's going to enjoy it.

"There's my girl! I missed you, love," he calls out, pausing as a few cameras flash. Passing his sign off to whomever stands beside him, he strides to me with long, purposeful steps, pulling me into his arms and smashing his mouth against mine.

Cheers and whistles erupt around us. Flashes blink like a strobe light against my eyelids. Frozen with emptiness, Corey molds my body into his, nipping at my bottom lip with more zest than necessary. I wince and he grins.

"Did you miss me as much as I missed you?" he asks, but I hear the threat behind his words.

When I don't respond, he pinches my skin underneath my sweater until I nod.

"She's speechless," Corey announces, laughing, the crowd following his lead.

His fingers dig sharper into my side until I'm grinning like a cartoon character, fake and plastic and overkill for the scene.

Corey leads me over to the baggage carousel and snaps his fingers at someone to gather my suitcases. Linking my fingers in his, he pulls me toward the exit, grinning for the cameras, for the people.

Panic begins to swell in my throat, entering my chest and squeezing against my organs until I think I'm going to explode. Black floaters appear in my line of vision.

Stop being his stupid puppet. Don't let him pull all the strings.

You've spent three months rebuilding yourself.
Don't collapse now.

"You landed early! I'm so happy you're back." Addison swoops into the airport, squealing as she throws her arms around me and pulls me from Corey's clasp. "We have so much to discuss for your Grand Ole Opry performance, and then there's your tour. Girl, do we have to get to work!" Addison speaks louder than normal, putting on a show for the cameras, pulling me from Corey without drawing suspicion. But under the thin veneer of her cheerfulness, I hear the concern. I note the daggers her eyes shoot at Corey.

"Come on, Addi. Everly's exhausted; she needs to come home and rest." Corey steps forward. "Jet lag is —"

"Part of the career of a country artist." Addi links her arm with mine, pulling me toward the exit. "Y'all can drop her suitcases in my car over here." She ushers me along, settling me into the front seat of her car and talking a mile a minute to all the people surrounding us because of the attention Corey's drawn.

His mouth twists, his eyes emitting pure hatred.

Offering him a small wave, I slip on a pair of sunglasses and close the passenger door. Addison slides into the driver's seat and flips the ignition. "You good, babe?"

"Doing the best I can." I admit, staring out the windshield. "Thanks for coming."

"As if I'd let Corey pick you up from the airport.

There's no way you'd be able to avoid him with so many curious eyes on y'all."

Plucking at my lower lip, I nod. "Now what?"

"Now, you gear up for your performance. You kick ass on tour. And you get the closure you need."

"EVERLY?"

"Yeah?"

"I'm so sorry, babe. I have to take this meeting. It's with this new duet who is making some serious waves. Leo and Lila, have you heard of them?"

"Nope." I respond, walking into Addison's kitchen. "Thanks." I grin at the mug of coffee she passes me. "But I'll check them out."

"You should. I think you'd really like their sound. Anyway, I'm meeting them at the office. I'm so sorry, I canceled all my other meetings for today and —"

"Addison, stop. You can't cancel your life just because I'm back. You should keep your work commitments. Honestly. You've already taken too much time off."

"Says you!" Addison laughs before pausing. She leans her hip against the kitchen counter and studies me. "You're different, Everly."

"I miss Aaron."

"I know, babe. But you're also stronger."

Nodding, I sip the coffee. "That's what I keep telling myself. Today, I turn on my phone and face reality again."

"You haven't turned on your phone yet? Everly, it's been three days!"

"I know. But you know how well I do denial."

Addison snorts, shaking her head. "Can I pick anything up for you on my way back?"

"Nope, I'm good. I think I'll head to the gym for a bit. See if Mark is there for a training session."

"You think that's a good idea?" Addison shoulders her purse, but her eyes stay trained on me.

I shrug. "I can't quit living my life either."

"I know. Just, be careful, okay?"

"I will. Have a good meeting, Addi."

The clip of her heels echoes as she walks to the front door and slips outside, locking the door behind her.

I spend some time lounging in the living room, drinking my coffee, and thinking about Aaron. And Olivia. I hope she's feeling better by now. I really need to turn on my phone and get in touch with Aaron. Let him know that this is for the best. That I need to confront Corey on my own in order to move forward with my life.

Jesus, how did I make such a mess of things?

Forcing myself to change into workout gear, I toss a pair of headphones and my phone into a gym bag, promising myself that I'll reach out to Aaron after my workout. Just need to clear my head first.

Stepping out into the breezeway of Addi's apartment, he moves faster than I ever gave him credit for.

"Where're you heading, love?" Corey's voice causes me to jump as I swing an arm in his direction. He chuckles, gripping my upper arm easily and using his other hand to catch the door before it can close behind me. "The gym? That's probably for the best, you've gained weight while playing house."

"Let me go or I'll scream." I tug at my arm.

Corey chuckles, clucking his tongue. "Come on, babe. We both know Addison left thirty minutes ago for a meeting. Leo and Lila are becoming a famous duet around here; she'd be stupid to pass up the opportunity."

"You planned it, didn't you?"

Corey shrugs.

Opening my mouth, I let out a piercing scream just as Corey shoves me backward, through the open door and into Addison's apartment. Stepping inside, he kicks the door closed behind him and leans against it. Folding his arms across his chest and crossing his ankles, he grins down at me, a wicked glint in his eyes. "We're going to play a game."

"Fuck you." I spit out from my place on the floor, scrambling to stand again.

"Ah, I see you're time abroad as made you feisty again. Just think how much fun it will be for me to break you once more."

Retreating, I look around for my bag, desperate to get to my phone.

Why the hell hadn't I turned it on yet?

Why didn't I have it in my hand in case I needed to make an emergency call?

"You used to be smarter than this, Everly." Corey chides, guessing at my thoughts. "You got lazy in Scotland."

Not lazy. Safe. I felt safe in Scotland and I let my guard down.

Stupid, stupid, stupid.

Taking a deep breath, I square my shoulders and remind myself that I can do this. I've spent the past three months building myself up. And countless months before that in therapy. I can confront Corey. I can take back my independence, my worth, my life. "It's good you're here, Corey. We should talk."

His grin grows as his eyes narrow. "Talk? Okay. Do you remember the rules Everly? For every lie you tell, I'll —"

"Coffee?" I ask, keeping my tone flat as I walk into the kitchen and pour two mugs.

End this. Stand up for yourself. Don't let him get in your head. Don't let him take your control. My therapist's voice sounds in my head and I know I can do this; I can stand up to Corey.

"Have to give you a consequence." He continues, following me into the kitchen, undeterred.

I sigh, leaning against the counter, the candlestick holders I bought Addison for Christmas last year at my back. "No game and no more rules, Corey. I'm no longer playing. We're over, done. I didn't come back for you."

"We'll never be done, Everly. Surely, you must know that." He cocks his head to the side, looking at me like I'm daft.

Every muscle in my body fires to life at his proximity, at his unwavering glance.

"Our careers are too intertwined." He steps closer, his pace slow, his voice deceptively soft. "Our lives enmeshed." He stops a few feet from me and pauses, letting out a long exhale. "I missed you, babe. Now, are you still planning to have a career, or are you too caught up in playing house with a man who will never love you the way I do?"

"Aaron loves me more than you can comprehend," I spit out, taking the bait.

Corey's hand is lightning fast when it connects with my cheek. The burn races through my body like adrenaline, spurring me on, even though I know better. Clenching my teeth, they rattle in my mouth, my eyes smarting with tears.

Don't let him get in your head, Everly.

"I'm sure he'd move on quickly if you keep packing on the pounds like this." His hand drops to my waist and pinches my side. "I'll call Mark. We'll get you in for two sessions a day until you look relatively fuckable again."

"Fuck you, Corey."

This time, his fist connects with my stomach and I

hunch forward, winded. It hurts, my god, does it hurt. But the physical pain Corey inflicts almost soothes the hurt my heart is grappling to process.

Almost.

"You know better than this, baby. Why do you do this to me? Question how much I love you all the time? You make things so difficult when they could be so perfect between us. We'll never be done. I'll never let you go. Ever. You made it hard enough with disappearing to Scotland, but even there, I found you." His fingers circle my wrist as he tugs me into his frame.

Wrapping his arms around me, the scent of his cologne mixed with the gin on his breath burns my nose. Vomit. I want to vomit. Struggling against him, I try to lift my knee to connect with his groin.

He chuckles, slamming my back against the counter and grasping both of my wrists in his large hand.

Over his shoulder, my gaze connects with Addison's mantle. With the framed photo of us from an awards ceremony.

I can do this. I can end it. Reclaim my life.

"How-how do you know so much about my time in Edinburgh?"

"Oh, baby, for such a smart woman, sometimes you really are stupid." Corey's mouth lifts in a lop-sided grin, his eyes glinting. "Think, sweetheart. How would I know about your comings and goings? Have the stock of photos I do? Who would know that information and be able to send it to me? Hmm?"

"Dan." The name leaves me on a strangled whisper.

"Good girl. Took you long enough to sort that one out. Then again, you always were a bit slow."

My heart stutters in my chest as a new wave of betrayal washes over me. How didn't I realize it sooner? Of course it was Dan. There is no one in my professional life, save for Addison, that Corey hasn't won over.

Corey's free hand strokes up and down my right side, his fingertips grazing over the scar he marked me with years ago. "I missed you, Ev."

In my peripheral vision, I glance at the heavy candlesticks. If I can just get my hand on one. Stay calm, stay focused.

My body stiffens, unyielding under Corey's touch as my mind focuses on what I need to do. I will no longer be a willing victim in Corey's sick charade. I will fight for myself.

I will fight.

Corey's chest presses into mine as he dips his head, running his nose along the shell of my ear. "I need you, Everly. Can't you see that?" His hand is a gentle caress as it cups my cheek, his thumb sweeping along my cheekbone.

I breathe shallow breaths, waiting for an opening.

The longer he gazes at me, the more his eyes narrow.

Until they're tiny slits of anger and evil.

"I need to fuck all of him out of you, make you

remember exactly who loves you best. It's me, Everly. It will always be me."

His caress turns painful as his fingers dig into my hair, pulling. He drops my hands as he grinds into me, pining me painfully against the counter top.

Shooting out an arm, my fingers collide with the candlestick and I swing it wildly. "I fucking hate you!"

But Corey is stronger, faster, meaner. He dodges the blow, slamming my hand into the counter until the candlestick falls to the floor. Yanking me to the ground, right in the middle of Addison's kitchen, he kneels on my thighs, anchoring me to the hard tiles. His hands are violent as they pull at my clothes, his eyes wild.

"Stop it!" I shriek, slapping at his hands.

The sound of his laughter washes over me, his heavy breaths like whips against my skin. "I need you back, baby. My Everly would never try to hurt me. I want my baby back." He growls, pulling my yoga pants down my hips. "You broke so many goddamn rules. All the fucking rules." His voice is ragged, tortured, as he rips my underwear to shreds. Peering at me for one blink, his mouth twists, before he plows into me.

I scream out in pain, my back arching off the floor, even as Corey's strong thighs press me down. An agony that is so much deeper than physical hurt burns through my chest. I lash out uncontrollably, punching Corey's chest, pounding at his arms. He captures my hands roughly in a fist and pins them above my head, rendering me immobile.

"Tell me you love me, Everly." He groans, his voice a mixture of pleasure and pain.

"I fucking hate you!" I buck against him, feeling violated and damaged and angry.

A glimmer of satisfaction flares in his eyes, causing my stomach to revolt. Bile snakes up my throat. *He likes this. He likes hurting me.*

"You're sick! Do you know that?" I scream.

"I missed you so much." He closes his eyes, pounding into me so hard, I feel my insides tear and bruise.

I scream every ugly word I can think of, tears spilling from my eyes and pooling in my ears. Struggling against Corey with all of my strength, he continues to move inside of me until he's spent and I'm broken.

Pulling out, he stands slowly. Glancing down, he spits on me and shakes his head in disgust. "He ruined you. Now, I have to retrain you all over again. Pack your belongings, I'll be back to collect you at dinnertime. You're coming home with me, Everly. You belong to me. We have work to do." Striding from the kitchen, I hear the front door close behind him.

I stay on the floor, feeling Corey's semen mixed with my blood drip out of me, watching the time turn gray. Did you know time has colors? It turns gray as all the hope from the past three months disappears and dread settles in its place.

With Aaron, I savored every moment.

With Corey, I pray for invisibility.

When I finally drag myself off the floor, my body aches and throbs. My skin is cold. My stomach empty. I feel like the shadow I used to be.

That's another funny thing about time. It can take long hours, difficult days, months of work to build yourself up. And only seconds to be torn down.

Wincing, I step into a steaming hot shower and wash the evidence of Corey's attack from my body. I dress slowly, the pain wrapping around me excruciating.

I need water and aspirin.

I need help.

I need to feel something.

Shuffling through my gym bag, I find my phone and turn it on.

21
aaron

Four days. That's how long Olivia is hospitalized.
Four excruciatingly long, difficult days.

Kate heads back to Spain after two days, after signing over her parental rights. Wiping at her eyes beneath large, black sunglasses, she kisses Olivia's forehead while she's asleep, slips out of the hospital room, and doesn't look back.

Me? I sit vigil. And I shut down everything that isn't about my daughter.

At least, I try to.

But inside, my stomach twists with concern for Everly.

My throat burns with rage over Kate's decision to leave.

My head aches with the internal vortex of emotions that I'm forced to ignore as I focus on my little girl.

Aunt Jenni spends long hours with me, reading aloud to Olivia, bringing me fresh clothes to change into, and making sure I eat.

Finn comes every day after work to distract me.

Daisy arrives each morning with coffee and polishes Olivia's nails.

Every single minute is agony.

Until Olivia is discharged.

Taking her home, I vow that from now on, she is my only priority.

MY PHONE RINGS in the middle of the night and I bolt from bed, praying it's Everly.

Seeing her name flash across the screen has me lurching forward, my foot still wrapped in the bedsheet, desperate to hear her voice. To know that she's okay.

"Lee?" I clench the phone to my ear, my heartrate spiking at the sound of her breathing on the other end.

"Aaron? Is Olivia okay?" Her voice is shaky, hoarse, as if she's been crying. It fills me with equal parts of relief and dread, an emotional cocktail I'm unprepared to deal with on top of everything else that's happened this week. My body and mind are wrecked after being consumed with agony over Olivia, with desperation for Everly, and with disgust for Kate.

Exhaling loudly, I drop my head back and close my eyes. "We got home from the hospital this morning. She's going to be okay. She's resting now. But God, she scared the hell out of me."

"I'm sorry she got sick. I'm so sorry I left that night.

I had no idea, honestly, I thought it was just a flu or some kid virus."

"Why'd you run, Lee?"

"Aaron, I — I'm sorry."

"I've been so worried about you. I kept calling and messaging. I even made Finn go by your flat to check on you. My daughter was in the fucking hospital, I'm dealing with stupid shit with her mother, and I'm distracted, thinking about you and if you ran back to the man who," I pause, nearly snapping my phone in anger, "who hurts you, Lee."

"I know." She whispers, defeated. "I'm sorry. I just, I just turned my phone on today and saw your messages."

I bark out a laugh, devoid of humor. "That's great, really fucking great. Hope you had a warm welcome back to Nashville."

"That's not fair. Aaron, I'm trying to do the right thing. I'm trying to protect Liv and —"

"I told you I had us. That I'd take care of Liv and you and me. That we'd be fine if we could figure it out together. You decided not to trust me. You're the one who left."

"I'm staying with Addison." Her voice quivers and it squeezes my stomach painfully.

"Just tell me, Lee. Are you okay? Be honest, do you need me? Is that why you're calling?"

Silence hangs between us, thick with unspoken words, heavy with messy emotions.

Everly clears her throat. "No." She murmurs. "I'm fine. I just wanted to check on Olivia."

A coldness sweeps through my veins at her words, tears pricking the corners of my eyes until they burn. "She's going to be okay. Thank you for calling." I reply in the politest tone I can manage. "Take care of yourself, Everly."

"You too, Aar."

Hesitating, I pause, so many words on the tip of my tongue.

I'm coming for you.

I miss you.

Don't do this.

We can figure it out.

But when I think about my daughter's tiny sleeping form one room over and let the gratitude I feel that she's okay fill my chest, I hold back. "If you ever need me, if you ever need anything, you call me."

"Good-bye, Aaron." Everly disconnects the call.

Tossing my phone down on my bed, I stand and shuffle to Olivia's doorframe. Watching her chest rise and fall, listening to the gentle snore of her nose, I thank God that she's okay.

And I remember that she's all I really need.

22

♫ everly 🎤

"How are you today, Everly?" Nicole, my therapist, asks as I sit across from her.

Shrugging, I pull the sleeves of my hoodie over my fingers and stare at the wall over her shoulder.

"Are you still living with Addison?"

"Yes."

"Have you told her about the attack?"

I nod, wiping at my eyes as tears leak out.

"I'm proud of you, Everly. Confiding in a friend is an important step."

"She wants to know why I haven't told the police."

"Why haven't you?"

I scoff, picking up a throw pillow and resting it in my lap. "You know why, Nicole. I'll be ruined."

"Do you really believe that? Do you really believe that by telling the police the truth about Corey, that you'll be ruined?"

"I'll lose everything."

"More than what you've already lost?" she asks gently and my chest aches as I picture Aaron's face.

God, do I miss him.

It's been six days since we've talked. And each day, the heartache I feel over letting him go increases. I thought time was supposed to heal wounds, not compound them.

"I need to hold onto my career." I mutter the excuse, but it sounds lame, even to me.

"Why do you think Corey would take that from you?"

Sighing, I pick at the fringe of the pillow. "I used to think Corey made me, that he created my career."

Nicole quirks an eyebrow.

"He didn't. I'm not saying he hasn't helped garner attention for my music or been important in my success, but he didn't create me. I did. I know that now. Since Edinburgh, since Aaron, I've realized that my life is mine and no part of it belongs to Corey."

"Then what's holding you back from pressing charges?"

"I'm scared." I admit, biting my lower lip. "I've been scared for so long that I let my fear dictate all of my decisions regarding Corey. But I came back here to stand my ground, to confront him, to get closure. I want to move on with my life."

"Will reporting Corey to the authorities help you move forward?"

"Yes." I whisper.

"What else?"

"I don't want to be scared anymore. I don't want to feel guilty and nervous and all of these negative things. In Scotland, I felt free. Weightless."

"Because of Aaron."

"Because of me."

Nicole smiles, leaning forward. "Forgive yourself, Everly. Forgive yourself and demand the closure you need."

"I MADE PASTA FOR DINNER."

"Oh, I love me some pasta." I hear Addison's keys hit the little dish on the entrance console moments before she enters the kitchen. "So, about the Grand Ole Opry..."

"Please tell me you were able to postpone it." I turn from the stove, clenching a wooden spoon in my hand. With everything that's happened since I've been back, performing in two days isn't something I'm looking forward to. Not when I'm about to press charges, not when I'm trying to pull my life together.

"Leo and Lila send you all their love." Addison snorts, toeing off her heels. "They are thrilled for the opportunity to fill in for you."

"Oh, thank God."

"You're sure you want to continue with the tour? We

can cancel, postpone, change dates. Whatever you need, Everly. You know that you're well-being is most important, right?"

Smiling at my best friend, I nod. "I do."

Addison chews the corner of her lip. "I know I pushed you over the last few months. About Corey, the Opry, coming home. I'm sorry, Everly. I just, I want you to do whatever you need to do for you now."

"Thank you, Addi." I turn, placing the spoon down on the counter. "But I want to go on the tour. I need it. For myself. But first, I need to get through tomorrow."

"What's happening tomorrow?" Addison frowns, slipping onto a barstool.

Pouring two glasses of wine, I pass one to her. "I saw Nicole this afternoon. I'm going to report Corey."

Addison's eyes widen and she places her wine glass down so quickly, wine sloshes onto the counter top. "Shut the hell up. Seriously? Oh, thank fuck, Everly. Tomorrow? Do you want me to go with you? Do you want to have the officer come to the house? What do you need?"

"I just, I need to do this. I need to start standing up for myself. Yes, tomorrow. No, I'll go to the station. Will you come with me?"

"Of course I will. Anything you need, I'm your girl."

"Tomorrow, then." I take a bite of pasta, closing my eyes and enjoying the taste. Corey rarely let me eat carbs and this dinner is one more reminder that I'm claiming back my life. Myself.

.....

23

aaron

"Read this." Daisy pushes into my office the next morning and places a coffee and her phone on my desk.

Lifting the coffee, I glance up at her.

"I'm serious. Check my phone." She urges.

Picking up her phone, my breath catches as I read the headline on the news source she's pulled up.

Country Music Producer Corey Hughes Arrested on Rape Charge

"Jesus Christ." I whisper to myself, scanning the article.

November 27 — Country Music Producer and Executive Corey Hughes was arrested early this morning after his longtime girlfriend, country singer/songwriter Everly Pierce, pressed charges including domestic abuse, aggravated assault, and rape. Hughes denies all allegations, but evidence provided by Pierce's camp proves otherwise.

At this time, representatives for Hughes and Pierce refuse to comment.

"He fucking raped her." I choke on the words, my eyes swinging up to Daisy.

She chews her lower lip, her eyes sad. "Did you know? About him?"

Dropping my face into my hands, I nod slowly. "It's why she left. He, Hughes, was following her and he sent her a photo of Livvy at ballet and, fuck, what a mess. She ran. I thought she ran back to him because she felt threatened but…"

"But she reported him." Daisy concludes.

"She pressed charges. I — I need to talk to her. See her. I can't believe, Jesus, I shouldn't have waited this long."

"Call her. And if you need to go, you know Finn and I will keep Olivia. Just, make sure she's okay, Aaron. No woman should go through shit like this. Especially not alone." Daisy's voice wavers and I wince, knowing how recent her own experience with a violent man was.

"Dais, I'm sorry, I didn't even think —"

"No, Aar, I'm fine. Really. Please, just call Everly." She smiles shakily and picks her phone up off my desk. "Good luck."

Before the door closes behind Daisy, I'm dialing Everly. My stomach twists in knots and my heart gallops in my chest. I need to hear her voice. I need to see her. I need —

"Aaron?"

"Lee, are you okay?"

"I'm okay."

"Brave girl. Please, please tell me that Hughes is behind bars."

"For the time being. I'm sure he's going to post bail, but he won't come anywhere near me."

"How do you know? How can you be so sure?" I feel like I'm going to throw up just thinking about Hughes being near Everly ever again.

Everly sighs. "I'm taking necessary steps."

"Such as?"

"Restraining order. Hiring a private security team. Doing what I need to do to stay safe. But not silent. I'm not doing silent anymore."

"Jesus. I fucking love you, Everly."

"I love you too, Aaron. I never stopped."

"I know, baby. I'm so sorry. Lee." I grip the phone tighter, not sure if I want to ask the next question or not. Fuck it, I need to know. "Lee, the charges you pressed, was it because of something in the past or more recent?"

Silence fills the line save for Everly's shaky breathing and the air I manage to pull into my lungs burns, blazing a trail of wildfire through my veins.

"He caught me off-guard a few days after I got back." Her voice is firm but monotone, detached.

"Everly, please, baby, please tell me he didn't —"

"He raped me on Addison's kitchen floor."

"Motherfucker." I pinch the bridge of my nose, dropping my head into my hand and trying to muffle the sob that breaks from my chest. My sweet, resilient girl was attacked just days after leaving

Edinburgh. She was right, I don't know Corey Hughes. I fucking underestimated him, and he hurt her. Again. Horror sweeps through me as another realization slams into me. "Shit, it was the day you called me, wasn't it?"

"I, I just wanted to hear your voice."

"Jesus, Lee, why didn't you tell me? I would have, I would have been there."

"I know. But you were right where you were supposed to be. Livvy needed you. How is she?"

"Full recovery. She's a little weak and tired still but growing stronger each day."

"I'm glad."

"Kate signed over her parental rights."

"No way. Wow, does Liv know?"

"Not yet. There's been a lot going on."

"Yeah." Everly snorts.

"How are you managing?"

"I'm okay. Taking one day at a time. Addison arranged for other artists to fill in for my Grand Ole Opry performance. I'm gearing up for my tour and then, then I think I'm going to take some time off."

"You're not cancelling the tour?"

"No. I want to go, to get out there and sing my heart out, to feel like myself again."

"Whatever you need, baby. But I'm waiting for you, Lee. I'm here and I'm not going anywhere. I'm not giving up on us. Do you understand?"

"Yes. I do. But I need to do this for myself."

"I'm proud of you. I've never been more fucking proud of anyone in my life."

"Call me when you're home from work?"

"Will you be sleeping?"

"Just call me."

"Okay, baby. I'll talk to you later."

"'Bye." She ends the call.

Sitting back in my chair, I rake my fingers through my hair. Then, I log into my computer and search for December flights to Tennessee.

DECEMBER 1 12:08PM

> Me: Happy December, love.

> Everly: Hey! Happy December. I bet it's much colder where you are.

> Me: Livvy is bundled up in a scarf, hat, and mittens. Only her nose is visible. What are you doing today?

> Everly: Appointment with Nicole and then meeting with my lawyer.

> Me: Corey?

> Everly: Out on bail.

Outrage rakes through my body as I reread Everly's

message, convinced that I'm seeing the words incorrectly. How the fuck is Corey already out on bail? What is wrong with the criminal justice system?

Dialing her, I sit back in my chair and clench my hand into a fist.

"Hello?" Her voice is breathy, laced with sleep.

"What the hell do you mean he's out on bail? That quickly?" I pinch the bridge of my nose, nausea churning in my stomach. I can't fly to Nashville until December 22 and the thought of Corey fucking Hughes getting near Everly makes me physically ill.

"Yes. Aar, relax. I'm okay." Everly breathes out.

"Lee."

"I swear. I'm meeting with my security detail right after my appointment with Nicole."

Blowing out an exhale, I grip the back of my head. "You trust these guys?"

"They're all former military, special ops. Yeah, I trust them."

"Okay. But if he so much as steps into the same building as you —"

"I promise, I'm going to be okay. We're going to be okay."

"Aye. I just hate feeling so helpless, so far away from you."

"February will be here before you know it. Livvy is going to love Florida. And all the Disney princesses."

Some of my anger recedes at the warmth in her voice. "Lee, I wanted to surprise you but —"

"Tell me!"

"I'm coming the 22nd."

"To Nashville?"

"Yep. Surprisingly, Kate's been better, more engaged, since signing over her parental rights. I'm not sure if it's because she doesn't feel so much pressure or what, but she really meant it when she said she'd see Liv over Christmas. She's going to take her to Glasgow to spend some time with her parents and family."

"Seriously? Oh my God! Aaron, this is going to be the best. I can't believe you'll be here for Christmas. I need to get a tree and do lights and —"

"Wait for me, love. We'll do it together."

"Wow! Okay, you've just given me so much to look forward to."

"Good. I can't wait to see you. Just, let me know how today goes, okay?"

"Promise."

"Love you."

"Me more."

Disconnecting the call, I stare at my blank computer screen, thrumming my fingers along the desk. Twenty-two more days.

It seems like eternity.

24
🎶 everly 🎤

K nowing that I'm going to be with Aaron in just over two weeks immediately brightens my outlook. Intent on keeping myself busy, especially with all of the media attention surrounding my opening up about Corey, I commit to extra time in the studio, additional workouts, and more choreography sessions. Add in my biweekly appointments with Nicole and social outings with friends who have shown me nothing but love and support, and the days pass by quickly.

"Drinks with Ginger and Grace tonight?" Addison asks, swiping my mug of coffee and taking a large gulp. "I'm already late for work and the day has barely started." She places the mug down. "Meet at Teddi's for happy hour?"

"Only if we're meeting for a girl's night. Not more chat about my tour branding." I quirk an eyebrow. I've been going full steam for the past week and could use a night to have a drink with friends that doesn't pertain to work, my image, or headlines.

Addi rolls her eyes but doesn't respond. Typical. "Have you read the news today?"

"Gah! No more headlines!"

"You want to read this one, babe." Addi grins, tugging on my ponytail. "See you for happy hour!" She calls out before the door closes behind her.

Do I want to read the article?

Since I pressed charges against Corey, an insane amount of media outlets picked up the story and ran with it. Every angle imaginable, painting me in various roles, has been covered.

I'm jealous of his success.

He's jealous of my success.

I cheated. He cheated.

He's a womanizer.

I made everything up to bolster sales.

Some articles were supportive and truthful, others were vicious and hurtful.

The good news: my career is still intact. I suppose the old saying that any publicity is good publicity still rings true.

The bad news: my emotional and mental stability swings like a pendulum from one hour to the next.

As usual, Corey's PR has tried to spin the narrative to show that I'm a jealous, insecure woman who needed more attention and made up a story to increase my sales before going on tour.

My PR team has been amazing in mitigating the media blows and has stressed that I need time and privacy. But if Addison is telling me to read an article, it's because she thinks it will help me.

Sighing, I pick up my phone and click on the article she messaged me.

Corey Hughes Hurt #MeToo

The headline causes me to jolt back, as if I've been punched.

What the hell?

December 8 — Since country superstar Everly Pierce pressed charges against music producer and executive Corey Hughes on November 28, a handful of women in the music industry have stepped forward with similar stories. Accounts of physical and sexual assault, intimidation tactics, and threats to ruin their careers are similar threads in each victim's story.

The undercurrent of fear to stay silent in the aftermath of assault is widespread and these strong, resilient, survivors are no different. But they're coming forward now, standing in solidarity with Everly Pierce, as she fights back against the man who repeatedly abused her during their four-year relationship.

My glance cuts to a timeline, outlining Corey's violent encounters with the women who have spoken up and my stomach heaves. Running to the sink, I throw up the breakfast I consumed. Hanging onto the countertop, I steady my nerves and turn on the faucet to rinse out my mouth.

Oh my God! I stop reading and stare at my coffee mug in shock. Corey hurt other women. He did this to other people. Before his time with me, during his time with me, and afterwards.

He's a monster.

My phone chimes with a text.

> Ginger: Thank God you said something Everly! Did you see how many women came forward because of your story?

> Andre: Hughes is scum. I'm proud of you, lady.

> Grace: I love you, Everly. I can't believe what you endured but your actions have inspired others! You're amazing!

> Addison: Did you read it yet?

Wiping a hand over my face, I reply to Addison.

> Me: Yes.

> Addison: So proud of you, Ev. I'll buy all your drinks tonight.

Snorting, I shake my head and sit back down.

For so long, for years, I've been too afraid to confront Corey. I thought if I reported him, it would mean the end of my career, of the life I built, of the dream I sacrificed for. Pressing charges against him, recounting my experiences with him to the police, was the most difficult thing I've ever done. I waited, scared out of my mind, for the backlash.

Sure, some people said hurtful things. Nicole advised me not to read all the comments on my social media accounts.

And yes, some people think I made the whole thing up.

But for some women, for some people in the world, my experience gave them strength, hope to know that they aren't alone, a platform to come forward and tell the world just how evil this man is.

And for that, I'm so grateful I finally stood up for myself. I'm relieved I claimed back my life.

Now, I can finally begin to move forward.

"BABE. Someone's at the door! Can you get it? I'm stepping into the shower. Just check first." Addison calls out.

Her overprotectiveness causes me to smile as I walk to the front door and peek out the window. My heart dips to my toes as butterflies take flight in my ribcage the moment I spot his blond hair. Aaron.

"You're early!" I pull the door wide open, watching the casual smirk on his face morph into a full smile.

"Missed you, Lee." He pulls me into a hug, and I wrap my arms around him. Breathing in the scent of his cologne, I relax and rest my head on his shoulder, pressing my cheek into the soft fabric of his sweater.

"What are you doing here?"

"Told you. I missed you." He kisses the top of my head and I pull back, grinning up at him.

"Come inside!" I pull him into the foyer. "Addi's taking a shower but she can't wait to meet you."

"Me too." He wheels his suitcase to inside the door and turns to face me. "Please tell me you'll stay with me at my hotel."

"Duh. I'm already packed." I bounce forward, pressing a kiss to his collarbone.

"I thought you said I was early." He chuckles, wrapping his arms around me and keeping me pressed against him.

"Aar, I've been packed since December 1."

Aaron laughs, squeezing me tighter. "Me too. Kate arrived a few days earlier than expected and asked if she could have more time with Liv so ... here I am."

"How's that going?" I step out of his embrace and tug on his hand, relocating us to the kitchen.

Aaron slides onto a barstool, his eyes darting around. "Nice place."

"I helped Addi decorate."

"Naturally." He grins before scrubbing a hand over his face, his eyes sobering. "Things have been okay. Kate's been a lot more communicative the past six weeks and has been checking in with Olivia more. We've explained to her that she's going to spend the year with me in Edinburgh so she can be with her friends and attend school and visit with her mum during school holidays like Christmas. I don't see the point in telling her about the custody arrangements now since she's so young and it seems like her life isn't going to drastically change. She'll still be with me in Scotland and visit with her mum when the timing works."

"Wow. That's, that's great that Kate is being more involved."

"Aye. I wonder if she'll change her mind in the future and want to play a more active role, and honestly, I'd be all for it. Things between Kate and me shouldn't affect Liv's relationship with each of us. I just want what's best for her, and she needs her mum."

"Of course. All kids need their mom and dad." I pour two mugs of coffee and slide one across the island countertop to him.

"And some are extra lucky because they have even more parents to love them."

Gripping the mug between my hands, I glance up. "What do you mean?"

Aaron sighs, a smile playing around the edges of his mouth. Pulling out a folded-up piece of construction paper from his pocket, he passes it to me. "From Liv."

Unfolding the paper, my heart thuds in my chest. Nerves skate along my spine. I have no idea why I feel so unsettled, but the truth is, I miss Olivia, and I want her and I to have a real, genuine relationship. As soon as I see the three stick figures, her and I in polka dot dresses, and Aaron in a blue shirt, I grin, tears pricking the corners of my eyes. "She drew us."

"Aye."

"But look what she wrote underneath." I add, turning the paper, so Aaron can read the word below the three smiling stick people.

Family.

"We are, you know?"

"I know," I whisper, pressing the picture against my chest. "Being with you is the only place that ever felt like home."

"I love you, Lee. And I'll fight alongside you every step of the way for however long this takes with Corey. Go on tour, sing your heart out, write the most beautiful songs, and be my family."

Rushing around the island, I throw myself at him and he scoops me into his arms. "I love you, Aaron. This time, I choose us."

Aaron's finger hooks under my chin and tips my face up toward his. Dropping his mouth, he kisses me. Soft and sweet. One. Two. Three times. "Good. Now, let me hear my song."

YOUR COUNTRY NEWS

Everly Pierce's New Single Hits #1 on Country Music Charts

January 18 — Everly Pierce has done it again! The thirty-four-year-old singer/songwriter is currently holding the number one spot on the Country Billboard Charts as well as Country Airplay and Top Country songs in both the US and Canada.

"Songbird" has shattered records, going viral within hours of being released. The song, based on Pierce's personal experiences of abuse with ex-Corey Hughes as well as healing alongside new love Aaron Anderson offers fans a glimpse into Pierce's emotional journey.

Currently on tour, Pierce is playing to sold-out shows in Chicago next!

Stay tuned for more country news.

Everly Pierce to Host CMA Awards

February 11— Country Music Star Everly Pierce will host the CMA awards this year. The "Songbird" singer has shattered records in recent months and is also on a sold-out tour. However, when we caught up with her earlier this week, she was delighted about the opportunity to host the CMA's.

"It's a dream come true. The past year of my life has been nothing but drama and it's so nice to have so many exciting things to look forward to. I love that the CMA's are in Nashville and I'll get to share the night with many incredible artists that mean so much to me." Pierce said.

Also joining her are Nashville's latest duet sensation, Leo and Lila. We'll have a full rundown of performances soon so check back for the latest country news.

Everly Pierce Announces Move to Scotland

March 23 — Last night, country singer/songwriter Everly Pierce announced that she will be moving to Edinburgh, Scotland upon the completion of her tour next month.

Pierce and her boyfriend, Scot Aaron Anderson, recently purchased a craftsman-style home in Nashville. Pierce plans to keep the home for when they visit the US, which, she assured fans, will be often. However, she will spend the majority of her time in Anderson's native Scotland.

See her Instagram announcement below:

@EverlyPierceSongbird: Hey there! I've got some super exciting news to share! My tour (which has been one of the most amazing experiences of my career) wraps up next month. And then, I'm moving. Any guesses where? If you guessed Scotland, you're right! Aaron and I have decided it's time to be in the same country. But don't worry, we're keeping a home base in Nashville and I'll be back for all the things. Much love for all your support! XO

Country Superstar Engaged to Scottish Marketing Guru

May 4 —Country singer/songwriter Everly Pierce and her Scottish boyfriend, Aaron Anderson, announced their engagement. The couple has been dating for nearly ten months and has overcome several hurdles during that short time including a legal battle with Pierce's ex, Corey Hughes.

Last week, the music producer and executive Corey Hughes was sentenced to six years in prison in addition to $400,000 in fines on sexual assault charges from nine women. He will serve his time at a federal penitentiary in Kentucky beginning next month.

Many of Pierce's fans have reached out via Instagram to wish her and Aaron congratulations. Although a wedding date has not been announced, Pierce shared on her social media that the wedding will "definitely take place in Nashville." Stay tuned!

EPILOGUE
🎵 everly 🎤

"Let me see your ring again." Daisy gushes.

"No, wait, it's your turn." I laugh, lifting her left hand and staring at the two-carat emerald cut diamond Finn placed there this morning. "I can't believe we're engaged!"

"I know, right? We can wedding plan together! This is going to be the best!" Daisy squeals, holding my hand next to hers. "I'm so obsessed with your ring too. I love the pear-shape. It's so you!"

"Aaron and Finn did really good." I admit, watching as our diamond rings throw the sunlight.

"So, southern weddings?"

"As if two southern girls would get married anywhere else."

Daisy and I laugh as Aaron and Finn exchange a look.

"You do know we're both getting married too, right?" Finn directs his question toward his fiancée.

"Yeah, yeah but you've already played your part.

Now, you just have to show up at the altar at the time I tell you." Daisy quips back.

Aaron laughs, clasping his brother on the shoulder. "Good luck with that, mate." He extends a hand to me. "Take a walk with me, love?"

Grinning, I place my hand in his, loving how his ring shines on my finger. Aaron pulls me up, wrapping his arms around me as we walk into the garden at Aunt Jenni and Uncle James's house.

"I can't wait to marry you, Lee." He says seriously, pulling me behind a tree to steal a kiss.

"Me too. Is next month too soon?"

"Tomorrow wouldn't be soon enough." Aaron's hands cup my cheeks as I hook my fingers around his wrists. "What kind of a wedding do you want?"

"Small, intimate, private."

"Sounds perfect." He kisses me again.

"In Nashville." I add.

"Whatever you want, love." Another soulful kiss.

"With Olivia as our flower girl."

"She'll love that."

Lifting on my tippy toes, I arc up to brush another kiss across his lips before I tell him the news. "And our baby as our secret guest."

"Great." Aaron answers, kissing me back and … freezing. He pulls back slowly, a confused kind of wonder shimmering in his eyes. "Wait what?"

Taking his hands, I place them on my abdomen,

pressing my fingers over his. "I'm pregnant, Aar. We're having a baby."

His eyes widen, his mouth falling open. A long exhale escapes from his lips before he whoops wildly, picking me up and spinning me around. "You're serious?" he asks, placing me on the ground, his fingers gripping my hips. "We're really having a baby?"

"We're really having a baby." I smile back. "And I can't wait to grow our family with you, Aaron Anderson."

Pressing his forehead to mine, Aaron smiles. "This is just the beginning, Lee."

THANK you so much for reading *This Time Around*. I hope you adored Aaron and Everly's story. Want more Scottish accents and second-chance romances?

DON'T MISS Lachlan's story, a Valentine's Day themed, first love, second chance novella, *One Great Love*.

Hey reader!

Thanks for reading *This Time Around*! I hope you loved Aaron and Everly's story. If second chance romances and Scottish accents are your jam, I've got more for you!

Read Lachlan's second chance at love here: *One Great Love*

Don't miss the novella that kicks off this series here: *My Christmas Wish*

Give Daisy and Finn's romance a read here: *One Last Chance*

Or meet Daisy's brothers in *The Kane Brothers Series*, a set of small town romances, here: *Rescuing Broken*

Thank you so much for your support. I'm so grateful you took a chance on my words!

XO, Gina

ALSO BY GINA AZZI

The Defender

The Heart Chaser

The Trailblazer (Nov 11)

The Hustler (Jan 6)

The Score Keeper (Mar 3)

Second Chance Chicago Series:

Broken Lies

Twisted Truths

Saving My Soul

Healing My Heart

The College Pact Series:

The Last First Game (Lila's Story)

Kiss Me Goodnight in Rome (Mia's Story)

All the While (Maura's Story)

Me + You (Emma's Story)

Standalone

Corner of Ocean and Bay

ACKNOWLEDGMENTS

Hey there!

Thank you so much for taking a chance on *This Time Around*! I loved writing this book and needed to give Aaron the happily-ever-after he deserved. I'm not sure if I'll continue writing in this world although I do have some lingering thoughts on Lachlan so you never know…

As always, so many wonderful people were involved in the creation of this book. Thank you never seems like enough but I'm so grateful to have such a supportive circle.

A huge thanks to Regina Wamba for creating the most amazing covers that always capture my characters perfectly!

Thank you to Rebecca Jaycox for editing this project and asking the tough questions that helped me develop Aaron's character.

So many thanks to Patrick Hodges for always being a sounding board, offering invaluable advice, and catching all the typos I miss no matter how many times I read the manuscript.

Thank you x a million to Melissa Panio-Peterson for

always listening, answering my crazy questions, and supporting each step of my journey! You are the best, lady!

To the fabulous ladies at Give Me Books Promotions - thank you for all of your hard work and help organizing all the things. I appreciate it so much and love working with you!

Shoutout and thanks to the members of Gina's Group for Book Gossip. I'm so grateful to you all!

To all the Bloggers, members of my ARC Team, and author friends (shoutout to YAAR and the OP) - thank you from the bottom of my heart for your constant support.

Sending so much gratitude and love to you, dear reader, for taking a chance on me and this book. Thank you for experiencing a love story with a slice of Scotland alongside me.

All my thanks and love to my world - Tony, Aiva, Rome, and Luna.

Happy Reading!

XOXO,

Gina

ABOUT THE AUTHOR

Gina Azzi writes Contemporary Romance with relatable, genuine characters experiencing real life love, friendships, and obstacles. She is the author of Boston Hawks Hockey series, Second Chance Chicago series, The Kane Brothers Series, Finding Love in Scotland Series, The College Pact Series, and Corner of Ocean and Bay.

A Jersey girl at heart, Gina has spent her twenties traveling the world, living and working abroad, before settling down in Ontario, Canada with her husband and three children. She's a voracious reader, daydreamer, and coffee enthusiast who loves meeting new people. Say hey to her on social media or through www.ginaazzi.com.

For more information, connect with Gina at:

Email: ginaazziauthor@gmail.com
    Twitter: @gina_azzi
    Instagram: @gina_azzi

Facebook: https://www.facebook.com/ginaazziauthor

Website: www.ginaazzi.com

Or subscribe to her newsletter to receive book updates, bonus content, and more!

www.ingramcontent.com/pod-product-compliance
Lightning Source LLC
Chambersburg PA
CBHW031026260626
47153CB00017B/2253